COME HOME TO THE COWBOYS
RETURN TO BLESSING, TEXAS
BOOK ONE

DAVIS, LACEY

Return to Blessing, Texas

Come Home to the Cowboys
Come Home to the Ranch
Come Home to the Lawmen
Come Home to the Country
Come Home to the Doctor's
Come Home to the Bride
Return to Blessing, Texas Books 1-3
Return to Blessing, Texas Books 4-6

Want to learn about my new releases before anyone else? Sign up for my New Book Alert and receive a complimentary book. Blindfold Me.

Secrets and the City Girl

New Yorker Kalie Parker is stunned to learn she has inherited the Sweet B Ranch in Blessing, Texas . She plans to sell the property as soon as possible. What would she do with a farm in the middle of Podunk? But what awaits her in the small town catches her off guard.

Preston Nash has lived in Blessing his whole life and worked at Sweet B since he finished college. He loves it here. Another ranch hand, Colby King, spent three years behind bars for a crime he would gladly do again if given the chance. When they meet the ranch's new owner, they are shocked beyond words.

Can the two cowboys convince this socialite from New York to move to the country and become a rancher? Or will she sell them all off without looking back?

A complimentary book is yours when you sign up for my newsletter on my website www. AuthorLaceyDavis.com.

CHAPTER 1

*K*alie Parker didn't know if she hated men or if she just couldn't find one that could satisfy her needs. None she'd dated gave her a sense of *I can't live without you.*

"How did the break up go?" her friend Stacy asked.

She gave a little laugh as she stood in front of the picture window on the tenth floor of her apartment building, talking on the phone to her friend. "I didn't have to say a word. He just understood and left. Do you think it's wrong of me to expect a man to take control in bed? Am I wrong for liking it a little rough?"

Her friend laughed. "No, but I think you're dating the wrong kind of men."

"Oh, so who should I be dating?"

"Maybe a construction worker or a cowboy. Someone other than the office types you've been going out with every week," she said.

"Oh yeah, I want to date a man with a tool belt hanging around his waist and every other word is a curse word."

Memories of the construction workers screaming obscenities that she did her best to ignore as she walked down the street came to mind. No, just no. She had imagined a handsome man with rippling muscles wearing a suit, but so far, she'd found none she wanted to know past the second date.

"Well, at least he would know how to use those tools hanging below his belt," her friend said with a laugh. "A good drill, a hammer, and maybe even some rope to tie you up with."

She laughed. There was that. "You are such a naughty girl who has deliciously wicked thoughts. It's been two years since I've found anyone to have sex with that I couldn't wait for them to touch me. Two frustratingly long years."

"You didn't have sex with this last guy?"

"Oh, hell no. We didn't last that long. There was no spark. Not even an ember when he touched me. And our dates were so boring, I couldn't imagine what he'd be like in bed. A real snooze fest. So no, I'm still in this long dry spell and I'm ready for it to end."

Sinking down into a chair, she picked up the mail and opened the envelopes, most of which were charity requests. But there was one large envelope from a law office in a place called Blessing, Texas.

What the hell was this?

"So are you going back to that dating site again?"

She sighed. "I don't know. Maybe I should look for something a little more risqué. Maybe someplace where the men are guaranteed to be manly, not wimpy."

"Good luck with that. Here in New York City, it's hard to find them unless they play professional sports. So many men work on Wall Street and, well, those suits look awfully nice, it's just when you peel back the layers, you find a wimpy white body that hasn't seen the sun in years."

Working from home every day, it was hard to meet good men she wanted to take to bed.

"Ain't that the truth," she said as she ripped open the envelope and started to read. Her heart skipped a beat and her breath seized in her throat.

"Stacy, listen to this," she said not certain if what she was reading was real. "Dear Miss Parker, we regret to inform you of the death of your grandparents. In their last will and testament, they left you the Sweet B Ranch in Blessing, Texas. If you do not wish to own the ranch, I have a buyer interested in purchasing the land. Please come to Blessing, Texas, in order to sign the paperwork. Your grandparents included a special request in the will that you remain at the ranch for two weeks before you decide to sell."

"Oh my God," her friend said. "Did you know about this?"

Sitting there stunned, she stared at the letter. It was official looking.

"No," she said. "All I knew was that my father had a falling out with his family before he married my mother. I didn't even know his parents were still alive or I would have gone and seen them."

When she cleaned out her parents' home after their deaths, there had been no pictures or anything about her father's family. On her mother's side, she had cousins, aunts, and uncles, but nothing on her paternal side.

"Where is Blessing, Texas?" her friend asked.

"I have no idea," she said, growing very intrigued. "Hey, I'm going to call the lawyer and see what he tells me."

The irritating noise of honking vehicles reached her tenth-floor apartment as she disconnected the call from her friend. It was still afternoon in Texas as she dialed the number listed on the letterhead.

"Nathan Alley's office," a young woman said.

"Hello, this is Kalie Parker. I received a letter from your office regarding land that my grandparents left me," she said.

"Just a moment and let me transfer you to Mr. Alley," the woman replied as Kalie's heart continued to hammer.

How had she never known about these people?

A few seconds later, a deep male voice came on the line. "Miss Parker?"

"Yes," she said. "I received your letter regarding the Sweet B Ranch. Can you tell me more about this land I'm inheriting? I knew nothing about the land or my grandparents."

There was a deep sigh. "I'm sorry to hear that. Your grandparents were lovely people. The Parkers were kind and helped so many people here in town. It's a shame they were no longer speaking to their only son. I always hoped for everyone's sake they would reconcile. Is your father still alive?"

"No, he died three years ago. Do you know what happened between my father and his parents?"

"No," he said. "When they came in and changed their wills several years ago, they told me they wanted you to inherit their ranch, but because they had never seen you, they asked that you come and stay for a couple weeks on the property."

That was odd. Why would they do that?

"Is there a house to stay in?"

"Yes, ma'am," he said. "It's one of the nicest ranches in our area. And believe me, the leaches are already sending me requests to buy the property. So you'll have no trouble selling it after your two weeks here are up."

Sitting there listening to the city noise, the thought of being in rural Texas for two weeks sounded heavenly. She could get away from the mass population and just enjoy the peace and quiet of the country before she sold out.

"What do you think the property is worth?" she asked curious as to what she was inheriting.

The man gave a chuckle. "Ma'am, I'm no real estate agent, but already you're receiving offers of two million dollars. The mineral rights have never been touched because your grandfather refused to let them drill on his land. Plus, I have a local developer who is wanting to put a housing subdivision there. If you sell, you'll be set for life."

A gasp escaped her. Speechless, she stared out the

window and knew she had to go to Texas. Millions, not hundreds of thousands. She would never have to work again if she sold the ranch.

"I'll book a flight and get out there as soon as possible," she said, flipping back her long dark hair. "Where should I fly into?"

"San Antonio, ma'am. We're about two hours west of the city. When you get here, call my office," he said. "Oh, and you'll probably need to stock up on some groceries in town before you head to the ranch. I think the maid threw out most of the food except for what was in the freezer. We have a small grocer in town where you can get fresh produce, milk, and eggs."

"Thanks," she said. "I guess I'll see you soon."

Hanging up, she glanced around her tiny apartment that cost her a mint. Why had her father kept this information to himself? Why hadn't she ever had the opportunity to meet her grandparents or visit the land and see where he came from?

Now they were all gone, but it sounded like they had given her a wonderful gift of owning a ranch. Sitting there, a myriad of tasks she had to do before she got on a plane filled her head.

Picking up the phone, she called her friend back, staring out the window and into the homes of strangers in the building across the street. At least they had the shades down in case they were strolling around naked again. The lights across the bay glittered like dying stars.

"I'm headed to Texas," she said. "Seems I've inherited a ranch."

"Ohhh, I'm so excited for you," Stacy said. "Maybe you'll meet a real-life cowboy. Maybe he'll rock your world."

The thought was tempting. She had not thought to ask if anyone was living at the ranch.

"Maybe," she said. "Couldn't be any worse than these Wall Street executive losers."

"What are you going to do with the ranch?"

She sat there a moment, pondering. "Sell it probably and then buy a nicer apartment."

Her friend sighed. "Or find a cowboy, have fantastic sex, settle down, and raise a couple of cowboys of your own."

That wasn't possible.

"I may work from home here, but my job wouldn't be happy with me living thousands of miles away from the office. That's doubtful."

"But hopeful," Stacy said. "I'd give anything to get out of the city."

From the time Kalie graduated from college, this was all she'd known. She'd grown used to the sounds of the bustling city even if she didn't love living there.

"It will be a nice vacation, and in the end, I hope I learn more about the people who are giving me their land. I'll be back in New York City and looking for a new place to live. And I'll once again go through the dating pool on one of the dating apps looking for Mr. Right."

"Or Mr. Right Now," her friend said. "Call me and let me know you're all right."

She laughed. "And if I'm not, are you going to fly out to Texas and rescue me?"

"Of course," she said laughing. "I just don't want you to fly to Texas and disappear, never to be seen again."

That wasn't going to happen.

"Even if I meet a handsome, hunky cowboy?"

"Even if," Stacy said. "Someone has to watch over you."

Warmth filled her chest. Stacy was her best friend and the only person who cared about her.

"Thanks, Stacy. I'll let you know what's going on when I get there."

CHAPTER 2

*P*reston Nash rubbed down the golden mare and wished for the hundredth time that he could afford to purchase the Sweet B Ranch. He'd worked here since he was sixteen. Sure, he'd gone away to college, but when he returned, he knew exactly what he wanted to do, and he adored the people he worked for.

Sadly, both Will and Lillian Parker had now passed and no one was certain about what would happen with their ranch.

The thought of finding another ranch to work on or even working on his family's ranch was not what he wanted. For some reason, this place felt like home, and if he had the money, he would buy the land. But the value far exceeded his million-dollar trust fund, and he wasn't going into debt for this place only to lose it later because of financial burdens.

The bunkhouse, his home away from home, was nice

with two bedrooms, a kitchenette, and a bathroom on the backside. He and Colby shared the space. They had done their best to take care of Mrs. Parker right up until the night she told them it was her time.

And sure enough, she'd died a few hours later, the two of them by her side with the hospice nurse. The Parkers were good people and it was a damn shame their family wasn't there when she passed.

"The stalls are cleaned and fresh hay has been put down for the horses," his coworker and close friend Colby King said. "Do you think we're going to get paid?"

"I have no reason to believe otherwise," Preston replied to his friend. "The Parkers took good care of us, and you know they wouldn't want their animals to be neglected, and I don't see Nathan, their lawyer, out here shoveling shit. Until he says so, I'm staying to care for this place. Or until the next owner takes over."

That was the problem. No one knew anything about who the Parkers had left the Sweet B Ranch to.

"I don't like uncertainty. It makes me want to run," Colby said.

"Rub down Sadie and maybe that will ease your anxiety," Preston told him. "Do you want to grab a beer tonight?"

Colby shuffled into Sadie's stall and pulled the brush from the nail it hung on then ran it down her spine. She gave a rumble deep in her chest in appreciation.

"No, I've got to go mail off the money to my parole officer. If you want me to, I could stop and pick up a six-pack at the store," he said.

"That's a good idea and maybe some hamburgers as well. I've got a hankering for a good hamburger," he said as his stomach grumbled in reply.

The man shook his head. "You're as bad as that fool on those Popeye cartoons about hamburgers."

"Yeah, so what?" Preston said. "Nothing beats a good hamburger."

The door to the barn flew open and Preston wanted to groan. The devil had just walked in wearing a black cowboy hat, crisp jeans, and an expensive shirt handmade to fit him with perfection.

The man looked like a million dollars but had the soul of a snake.

"You boys keeping things going here?"

"Yes," Preston said curtly. Short and precise answers would hopefully have the unwelcome visitor crawling back to whatever hole he slithered out of.

The man glanced around, staring up at the rafters of the barn. "This place has been here a long time. Did you know that my great-great-grandfather tried to purchase the place from Lillian Bradley years ago?"

"No," Preston said, not looking at the man.

Colby didn't say a word. Nothing. Just continued to rub down his horse.

"The woman was all alone and refused my grandfather. She refused to sell the place and married two Texas Rangers."

That was all interesting and such, but he wanted this snake out of the barn before he scared the horses.

"What can I do for you, Mr. White?"

The man grinned like he knew they were trying to get rid of him.

One of the horses snorted like it was growling for him to stay away.

"What's the lawyer telling you, boys? Have you heard who inherited the ranch?"

Like anyone would tell the hired hands anything.

Colby raised his head over the stall and glanced at the man like he was a total idiot. "We're to be out of here in fifteen days. They're giving us all a bonus of ten thousand dollars and telling us to move on. Also we can choose which horses we want to take with us and Rusty the cow dog will go to one of us."

"Really," the man said. "I hadn't heard they sold the place."

Rolling his eyes one final time, Colby bent to run the brush down the horse's legs.

"We haven't heard a thing," Preston told the man. "We're just doing our jobs until someone tells us to move on."

The man frowned and spit tobacco juice toward Colby.

"Why did you lie to me, boy?"

His head popped back up and he glared at the man. "We're the hired help. If you want to know the truth, I would suggest you speak to the Parkers' lawyer in town."

"I want this ranch. It should have been my family's

years ago and I aim to make certain that it becomes mine this time. If you'd been honest with me, there might have been jobs for the two of you."

Like he would ever work for this scum of the earth.

Neither Preston nor Colby acknowledged the man's words.

"Well, I would have thought you would like to have a guaranteed job," he said.

There was no guarantee with this man. He would hire you one day and fire you the next. Preston had seen him do it to men in the past, and he wanted no part of his operation which often skirted the edge of the law.

And he knew Colby would never take a chance on working for a man who didn't tread carefully on the up-and-up. The man didn't want to return to prison.

"Glad you came by, Mr. White," Preston said, hoping he would get the hint to leave.

"I'm meeting with the lawyer tomorrow to put in another offer on this property. I'm hoping this one will be the one that convinces whoever it is to accept that I'm going to purchase this land," he said, standing with his hands on his hips like he was directing traffic and telling them what was going to happen.

"And what will you do with the land?" Colby said, popping up from the stall and gazing at him like he wanted to throw a punch.

"The Big W Housing Development," he said with a grin. "New homes for anyone who would like that country atmosphere with city streets. Five-acre mini ranches."

Mini ranches? Just what the town of Blessing didn't need.

Colby shook his head and went back to brushing Sadie's thighs.

"What? You boys don't approve?"

Preston glared at him. "No, I don't. This ranch has really nice grasslands with rolling hills, perfect for cattle. Why divide up the land and sell small parcels to home-owners who will soon learn they don't like living where pizza can't be delivered."

The man grinned a cocky smile that made Preston want to punch him.

"For the money, of course," Jim said. "It's all about the money."

A growl came from the horse stall and Preston knew it wasn't an animal but Colby. The man was close to the breaking point, worried about losing his job and hating the fact that the Parkers who had taken in a convict and helped him find room and board and a decent wage were now gone.

It was time for the man to go. "Good afternoon, Mr. White. Don't let the barn door hit you in the backside on your way out."

The man knew he had gotten to them and his grin grew even wider.

"Enjoy the land while you can," he told them. "Because soon, you'll be drawing unemployment checks."

Colby jumped up, and Preston knew if the devil didn't

leave now, he'd soon have a black eye. Seeing the expression on Colby's face, Mr. White hurried out of the barn.

Once the door closed, a groan came from Colby. "Greedy son of a bitch. I'd like to take him behind the woodshed."

Unfortunately, Preston felt the same way. Glancing at his friend, he shook his head. "Let's just hope the new owner doesn't agree with him and decides to keep the ranch. That would definitely ruin all his plans."

"From your lips to God's ear," Colby said. "Now I'm going to head to town to get us that beer and run by the post office. Oh, and pick up two juicy hamburgers."

Preston grinned. "I'll be here waiting. Maybe we can watch a new episode of Yellowstone. I'm dying to know what happens next."

"Sounds like a plan. I'll be back soon," he said, walking out of the stall. Colby picked up his cowboy hat and headed toward the door.

"Colby," Preston said, hoping his friend knew better, but just wanting to warn him all the same, "leave Mr. White alone. Let the lawyers and the new owners figure out what to do."

With a sigh, he opened the door, letting a beam of sun light up the space. "Not even that asshole is worth going back to prison for."

CHAPTER 3

*A*fter Colby pulled into the lot of the local grocery store, he parked his Harley and then climbed off the bike, pulling off his helmet and locking it down. The motorcycle had been his one and only extravagant purchase since he'd gotten out of prison two years ago.

Even a bad boy needed something to keep him going. Some kind of incentive to keep the demons at bay.

He ogled the sight of a dark-haired woman in a pair of jeans clinging to her well-defined bottom and long legs walking into the store. The swing of her ass left him breathless.

"Well, well, well, what do we have here?" he said out loud to himself.

His body hardened at the sight of her, his breathing becoming shallow, and he groaned.

How long had it been since he'd noticed a woman in town? Hell, since he'd noticed a woman, period? Too long.

Maybe he needed a little diversion from the tension at the ranch. Would she be willing to spend a little time with him beneath the sheets?

Never before had he been so attracted to a woman. Sure, he'd seen women in town, but not like this. This woman had his heart racing and his balls tightening.

The traffic noise from the street didn't even penetrate his brain as he walked across the parking lot, only knowing that he had to follow her inside. See if he could catch a glimpse of her face. Her eyes. Her lips. Her breasts.

He hurried into the bustling store, racing up to talk to her. Just as he reached out to touch her shoulder, she stopped and bent over to pick up something and he ran smack into the back of her, his jeans-clad penis sliding against her tight pants.

A rush of desire swept straight through him to his cock and his heart. Dear God, what was he doing?

"Oh," she said, standing and turning, her large emerald eyes flashing annoyance.

"Sorry, ma'am," he said. Damn, he'd probably frightened her, and she now thought of him as some sexual pervert. Maybe he was, but he'd enjoyed the feel of her buttocks against his cock.

Her emerald eyes flicked over him and he smiled, wanting to know more about this woman. There was something about her slim figure, full breasts, and shapely ass that had him harder than a softball in a baseball cage.

Blessing wasn't exactly a large town and he'd never seen her before, but he wanted to see her every day now.

17

A frown graced her face and she turned away.

"I'm sorry, ma'am, can you tell me where the butter is?" he asked, wanting to prolong her leaving.

"I have no idea," she said, grabbing a basket and walking deeper into the store.

Obviously, she didn't like the fact that she'd gotten an up-close-and-personal feel of his rock-hard cock. But it wasn't on purpose.

He followed her, enamored by the way she looked, the smell of her, the sway of her hips, and those gorgeous breasts.

"Stop following me," she said, not even looking at him.

"Darling, I'm just doing my shopping," he said. "If you know where the butter or the beer is, I'd be happy."

Of course, he knew exactly where they were, but he was going to spend some time following her and maybe even try to get her to have dinner with him. This was one he wasn't willing to let get away.

"You're probably married," she said. "Does your wife know you act like this?"

"I'm not married. I'm sorry that I ran into you, but you're the one who bent over in the aisle," he said.

"Do your eyes not work?" she replied, still looking straight ahead and not acknowledging him.

"Oh, yes, ma'am, they work just fine. But I was looking up, not down, and then suddenly there you were in my path," he said, knowing even if he had seen her, he would have taken advantage of the opportunity.

Just then they arrived at the refrigerators that held cold alcohol.

"There's the beer," she said. "Now go away."

"Thank you," he replied.

She reached in and grabbed a bottle of Pinot wine.

"You drinking alone?"

"That is none of your business," she told him not looking at him.

He moved in behind her, and when she straightened, he was standing right there. Not touching her, but close enough she knew he was there and he could smell the sweet scent drifting from her.

"Have you ever had beer poured over your naked breasts, in your belly button, and then the cold brew poured between your legs? I love to sip my beer from between a woman's thighs."

She gasped and glared at him, mouth hanging open.

Maybe telling her what he was thinking wasn't such a great idea. Her body stiffened and those emerald eyes of hers glistened with fury.

Her eyes narrowed. "The butter is straight ahead. Now get out of my sight before I call the store manager."

Maybe he was a glutton for punishment, but he just couldn't help himself. He was obsessed with this woman.

"Thank you," he said. "It would taste mighty fine on a baked potato along with a grilled steak. Would you have dinner with me?"

"Are you serious?" she said. "You've overstepped my boundaries and I don't sleep with someone on the first date. Or the second or even the third. So get the hell out of my way."

Yes, he was pushing the boundaries, but the way that cute little T-shirt clung to her breasts all swelled up and her nipples protruding like headlights made him forget himself. He wanted to pull her bra down and taste those sweet orbs of hers. They would be sweeter than honey.

Shocked, he realized no woman had affected him this way since high school. What the hell was he doing? And yet he couldn't stop himself.

"Darling, I'm willing to wait for you. I think you'd be worth it," he said softly. "Your time, your space."

Rolling her eyes, she turned and walked away.

"What's your number? I'll call you," he hollered out.

Turning back, she shook her head and kept on walking. Then she raised her hand and flipped him off.

A grin spread across his face.

The woman had spunk, and he liked his women to have lots of spunk. Lots of fire in that one and maybe that's what drew him. He needed a woman who could accept his desire for control in the bedroom. The way he liked his sex was a little rough. He would turn her over his knee and show her who was in charge.

He didn't want to seem like a stalker, so he let her walk away, but somehow he was going to find her again.

Right now, he couldn't wait to get home and tell Preston all about this mysterious woman he'd met in the grocery store. She had to be from out of town. He just hoped she wasn't passing through. Tomorrow he'd check out the local hotel and see if she was staying there.

The thought crossed his mind to follow her, but he feared that would just frighten her.

After paying for his groceries, he walked outside and studied the car she'd gotten out of. Looking it over, he noticed it was a rental vehicle.

Damn, she was probably just stopping for snacks before leaving Blessing in her rearview mirror.

Climbing onto his Harley, he started up the motorcycle and pulled out of the parking lot. If nothing else, he'd had an interesting trip into town.

After sliding through the one-lane drive-thru for dinner, he gave the beast between his legs more gas and shot down the road toward the ranch.

This was where he belonged. Will and Lillian Parker had taken in the cynical, angrier-than-shit man who'd just gotten out of prison. They'd trusted him and told him that as long as he didn't drink too much or do drugs, treated their animals with respect, and worked hard, he would have a home here. And they'd kept their promise right up to the day they died.

Oh, how he hated that day. First, Will, and then several months later, Lillian. Now he didn't know what was going to happen with the ranch or himself, for that matter.

Lord knew he was not going back to his home in Louisiana where he'd known nothing but heartache. Not even for his mother.

The woman had made her choice and she now had to live with the situation.

Giving the rocket between his thighs more gas, he leaned back and let the wind blow through his hair. He often didn't ride without his helmet, but sometimes a man just needed to let the wind cool him off.

And after seeing that gorgeous woman, he was hot and bothered and so ready to fuck.

With the turnoff to the ranch coming up, he slowed and then carefully made his way along the dirt road.

When he pulled up to the barn, Preston was sitting outside near a fire he'd built in the pit not far from the main house. After the Parkers had died, they'd taken to using the fire pit whenever it was nice to sit outside, as long as the skeeters didn't try to carry them away.

"About time you got back with those burgers. I'm starving," Preston said.

"You are not going to believe what happened at the grocery store. I ran into one snooty, beautiful bitch. Unfortunately, she's from out of town, so I don't think I'll see her again, but if she'd said yes, you'd be having your hamburger for breakfast," Colby said.

Preston grinned. "Damn, it's been so long since we've shared a woman."

"I know," he said, pulling out the beer, setting it down, and then grabbing the burgers. They were probably a little on the cold side, but still that would be better than anything they could fix.

"Did you at least get her name?"

"Nope, she told me to go away or she was going to contact the store manager," he said with a grin.

Preston laughed. "That's certainly wooing a woman."

For the next five minutes, Colby told Preston about the woman and how he'd run into her back end. God, that had felt so good.

"You really are wanting some woman to file charges against you," Preston said laughing.

"It was an accident. A good accident, but I didn't mean to," he said, the memory still fresh, his cock still pulsating at the feel of her firm backside.

"Please tell me you didn't follow her out of the grocery store."

"No, I didn't want to scare her. I just wanted to get to know her, maybe fuck her if she was willing," he said, leaning his head back against the lawn chair, remembering how she'd reacted when he told her he wanted to drink beer from between her thighs.

The thought of pouring cold brew over her and slowly lapping it up made him sigh.

They sat there staring at the flames, drinking, and eating their cold burgers.

"Do you ever think about getting married? Settling down?" Preston asked. "I'd like a wife and family."

Colby sighed. Preston knew some of his story, but there was so much he kept buried inside that he didn't want anyone to know about. Looking back, he shouldn't have stolen that car but still ran as fast as he could.

What did he have to offer a woman? With his upbringing, there were no guarantees that he would be a good father. He'd never had a good example, and his mother...It was a wonder he even thought about women.

"Nope," he said, coming to the conclusion. Marriage and families didn't go with men like him.

And he would never subject any child to striped legs and bruises like he'd endured. How his teachers could live with themselves he didn't know, but no one had come to his rescue. No one. Not until he met the Parkers.

Maybe his reaction to this woman was because of all the uncertainty in his life since the Parkers abandoned him. After what he'd lived through and endured, he liked his life to just hum along. Living out here was quiet and there were few people and no problems.

A woman would definitely screw that up.

Just then the sound of a car turning down the lane had them rising from their chairs and glancing down the dirt lane that led to the house to see who was coming to visit. If it was that Jim White again, there would be trouble.

The color of the car was the first thing Colby saw.

"What the hell?" he said.

Staring at the rental car, his insides began to shake. "Oh no. No."

"What?" Preston asked.

"I recognize that car," he said. "You don't think she's the new owner do you?"

Just then the car pulled to a stop and the gorgeous dark-haired beauty stepped out of the vehicle.

Preston gasped and said in a low voice. "Dear God. No wonder you're horny."

"Hello," she called. "I'm looking for Will and Lillian Parker's home. Is this it?"

"Yes, ma'am," Preston called out. "You're at the right place."

They both stepped toward the light where she could see them.

Suddenly she gasped and he knew she'd recognized him.

"You," she said.

"Yes, ma'am," he said politely, taking his cowboy hat off. "Colby King. I'm one of the ranch hands here."

"Preston Nash," his friend said, stepping up and shaking her hand. "Welcome to the Sweet B Ranch."

"Dear God," she said, glaring at Colby. For the first time in years, he was afraid he was about to be fired.

CHAPTER 4

*I*t was that handsome jerk from the grocery store. Never before had she been so openly accosted and yet, the sight of those big, burly arms was tantalizing. The tattoo on one arm and the curl of his thick lips had left her imagining things she'd never thought of. But she didn't know the man, and now here he was standing in front of her with a beer and his hat in hand.

The beer he'd wanted to trickle down her body and taste her. The thought had conjured up all kinds of images that left her body warm, but he was a complete stranger. A man who looked dangerous and foreboding.

"Can we help you unload the car?" Preston asked.

"Yes, please," she said. "It's been a really long day, and some jerk at the grocery store tried to pick me up."

A snicker came from Preston.

"Sorry, ma'am," Colby said, smacking Preston on the arm.

She popped the trunk of the car. "Someone grab the suitcases and I'll take the groceries."

The two men rushed to do her bidding, and she couldn't help but smile. When she reached the door, she pulled out the key the lawyer in town had given her.

It was an old-fashioned lock and she struggled to open the door.

"Here, ma'am, let me," Preston said.

The man smelled of leather as he set her suitcase down and took the key from her. Their hands brushed and a tingle of awareness spiraled through her. What was wrong with her today?

The big cowboy jostled then unlocked the door. Pushing it open, he waited for her to step inside.

From the dirt lane, the house had looked beautiful. Inside it was dated, but still a very nice home.

She walked through the house until she found the kitchen and set the groceries down. The two men took the suitcases up the stairs. She wasn't about to go exploring until after they'd left.

In a moment, they hurried back down, their boots clunking on the wooden stairs.

"How did you know the Parkers," Colby asked.

She sighed. She would never understand why her father had not introduced her to her grandparents.

"My father was their son," she said.

The men glanced at one another and frowned. "They had a son?"

A little laugh escaped from her. "Yes, though I didn't

know about them, and he never mentioned his parents. Always told me his family was dead."

Shaking her head, she glanced around. "I would have loved to have met them."

"They were the kindest people," Colby said.

"Yes," Preston agreed. "Everyone in town loved them except for Jim White."

If she hadn't been so tired, she would have asked about Jim White, but right now, she didn't care. Food and a bed were all she was interested in.

She walked around the main room and gazed at the pictures on the mantel.

"Nothing has been touched since they died," Preston said. "Will died about six months ago and Lillian a month ago. We miss them something fierce."

"Their partner, Ben, died at least ten years before," Colby said. "I never met him."

Partner? She'd not heard that they had a partner in owning the ranch. That seemed odd.

"Where did you come from?" Preston asked.

With a laugh, she couldn't help but think how different her world was compared to this place.

"New York City," she said. "My job took me to the Big Apple."

The two men glanced at one another.

"Sooo, you don't know much about ranching," Preston said.

"Not a thing," she replied.

Colby leaned against the window and gazed out. "This ranch is a wonderful place. It's made your family a lot of money over the years, working cattle and horses and even a few pigs. Your grandparents were so proud of this land," he said, not looking at her.

The man had lost his flirtatious manner and was now almost remote, even a little cold.

"Sadly, I know none of the family history. My father never mentioned this place. I knew he grew up in Texas, but he always said he would never step back into this hell hole."

Turning from the window, Colby shook his head.

"It's not a hell hole," he said. "It's a great place to live and work. A wonderful place to raise a family."

Preston gave Colby a strange glance.

"Where are you guys from?"

"Raised here all my life. My family owns the ranch a mile down the road. We've been here since the beginning. I'll never leave," Preston said.

She smiled and thought about how she couldn't wait to leave Connecticut and was thankful for the job she had in New York City. But then growing up with a very strict father had not been easy.

Colby had not replied. He hadn't told her about coming to Blessing or if he'd lived here forever.

"I guess there could be worse places to grow up," she said. Glancing down, she frowned. "Did you guys put my laptop case upstairs?"

"That flowered bag?" Colby asked.

"Yes, that one," she responded. "Tomorrow I have to check in and do some things for work."

"Yes, ma'am. It's up in the bedroom. We put you in the master bedroom."

"Thank you," she said and then glanced at the door and back to them. She'd been up since five this morning to catch her flight and then the two-hour drive from San Antonio. She wanted to eat a quick bite and crawl into bed.

Tomorrow would be soon enough to learn more about her family and the ranch they owned. Even these two cowboys.

"Nathan had the house cleaned and there should be fresh sheets on the bed," Preston told her.

The man he mentioned was the attorney she'd met this afternoon. They were going to sit and talk in the next few days. But first, she wanted to learn as much as she could about her grandparents. She wished there was someone who could tell her why her father no longer acknowledged his parents. But she would have to wait and see.

"We better let you go and get some rest. If you need anything at all, just call us," Colby said.

"And how would I do that if I don't have your number?"

A grin spread across his face and she knew he was thinking he was going to get her number. She was too tired to fight him and just as soon as she left this two-bit town, she'd be blocking him.

The man handed her his cell phone. "Call me."

She glanced up and frowned at him as she took the phone. "I'll give you my number, but I'm not going to have dinner with you. I'm not going to let you pour beer all over me, and no, we won't be sleeping together."

Preston slapped a hand over his mouth, failing to stifle a gut-busting laugh.

"Strictly business," Colby said with a straight face and a nod. "And be sure to get Preston's number, as well."

After they had exchanged cell numbers, she opened the door and swept her arm through the air toward outside. "Goodnight, gentlemen. It's been a long day. We'll talk more tomorrow."

She was certain they were anxious to learn her plans for the ranch. In two weeks' time, she hoped to have this place sold and be driving the rental car back to San Antonio where she would catch a plane back to civilizations. Her ordinary, boring world, where the men wore suits, not jeans and boots or had arms that bulged with muscles.

"Goodnight, ma'am," Preston said at the door.

It was then she realized she had not told them her name.

"Kalie," she said. "Kalie Parker."

Preston grinned and walked out.

"Again, my apologies, Miss Parker," Colby said. "Don't know what came over me 'cept that you are one fine-looking woman and I'm just a lonely cowboy."

With a sigh, she realized she was going to need these

men and it would be in her best interest to stay on their good side.

"Apology accepted," she said.

"Goodnight, Kalie," he responded.

For a moment, she was tempted to tell him to call her Miss Parker, but she didn't. Instead she closed the door behind him and slid the door lock.

Glancing around the house, she began a thorough inspection. The home was large, and while it was outdated, it had good bones. Good structure throughout. She would get a pretty penny for this place. It would be a great home to raise a large family in.

Oddly, it had character all its own that she kind of liked. A homey feeling where she could see a large family gathered around the dining room table with a Christmas tree reaching up to the second floor in the main room and children chasing each other through the house.

Going up the stairs, she checked each bedroom until she found the master.

There in the center of a very large room was a bed big enough to hold four or five people.

"Why did they need such a large bed?"

Were they big people? She would be lost in that monstrosity.

A brick fireplace stood against one wall and framed pictures sat on the mantel. In one, she saw the face of her father.

She picked up the frame and stared at the boy. Her father had to be about eight years old and he stood between two smiling men. One she recognized by family resemblance as Will Parker, his father. The other man she didn't know.

"You were here, Daddy," she said. "Why didn't you tell me about your parents? What were you hiding?"

CHAPTER 5

*A*fter the door closed behind Colby, the men walked through the night to the bunkhouse, their boots crunching on the gravel of the drive.

An owl hooted off in the distance and a cow mooed in the pasture. The sounds of home.

As soon as they were far enough away that he didn't think they could be heard, Preston swore under his breath.

"Damn, Colby, she's a stunner. No wonder you acted like a fool," Preston said, wondering how he would have reacted to seeing her traipsing into the grocery store.

"Well, it almost got me fired," he said. "She didn't threaten, but I could see it there in those titillating emerald eyes. Now do you understand why I want to fuck her?"

Of course, he did.

"Oh, yes," Preston said, walking into the bunkhouse. "But how long is she going to stay? And what's she going to do with the property?"

So many questions swirled in his mind now that the new owner had finally arrived.

The woman had not said a word about her plans except that she intended to return in two weeks to the big city. Two weeks they had to convince her to stay. Not to sell the land. And yet, he didn't want to put any kind of pressure on her.

Whatever they did had to be subtle. This was her decision. A bad owner who hated the ranch would be even worse than a new owner who wanted to make the land into a ranching subdivision.

"Damn, I wonder if she would sell the property to me?" Preston said, thinking out loud. All he had was his trust fund, and while he didn't want to carry a mortgage, it would be better than the land going to Jim White. Or maybe his parents would agree to help him.

That would have the family owning two large ranches in the area. But his father was one tight man when it came to his cash.

"I'd do everything I could do to help you, brother. But my funds are still in the building-a-nest stage."

Colby came from nothing and was slowly trying to save money, but as ranch hands, they weren't paid a big salary, just enough to get by. Of course, Mrs. Lillian had bequeathed to them each a nice bonus for helping her run the ranch after her husbands died.

Nathan had told them just as soon as the will was probated and the land sold, they would receive a lump cash sum. How much he had no idea. But probably not enough to buy this property.

Walking into the living area of their small home, they both sank into chairs. Normally, they watched television and then went to bed, but tonight was an exception.

Tonight, their world had been impacted by a beautiful brunette with flashing emerald eyes and lashes that seemed to sweep into next week.

"I guess we'll soon know her plans regarding the ranch," Colby said.

"Yes," Preston acknowledged. "But, damn, that woman is stunning. If only we could show her the true meaning of Blessing, Texas. Of our traditions and beliefs."

Colby chuckled. "I'm afraid I ruined that for us. But I'm glad now you understand."

Oh, yes, Preston had taken one look at her and wanted to roll her back onto the top of that car and taste those luscious breasts that were calling to him. Yank down her jeans and sink himself deep within her.

But he was a gentleman, and a good man didn't act on his baser instincts until the woman said yes.

"When is your sister getting married?" Colby asked.

"In a week," Preston replied, his heart warming. Hard to believe his little sister was marrying her men. They were stand-up guys and she would be well taken care of. Her two husbands would not allow anything bad to happen to her. All Preston wanted was her happiness.

"What if we invited Miss Fancy Pants to go with us to the wedding? Then she could get a real idea of what

Blessing is like. Maybe, somehow, we can convince her to stay and not sell the ranch," Colby said.

If only. But that girl from New York was used to a much different kind of life. The hustle and bustle of a large metropolitan city. Not the quiet and peacefulness of the country. She probably thought they were hicks even though Preston had gone to college.

But he'd returned home just as quickly as he could. And yes, he enjoyed being a ranch hand. He knew all the procedures for running a successful ranch operation, but he hadn't been able to put his learning to use. Not yet.

The Parkers were old fashioned and he respected their wishes. But if he could, he would carry this ranch or his own into the next century.

"What if we took her horseback riding and showed her the ranch?" Preston asked.

Colby laughed. "Does she even know how to ride a horse?"

There was that. But he would gladly teach her.

"Don't know, but I guess we can find out. If not we'll put her on the tamest horse we have."

"Or she could ride with one of us as we showed her the ranch," Colby said. "Snug and safe up against my cock."

Preston laughed. "I don't think that's a safe place at all."

"No, but it's a satisfying place," he said grinning.

They sat for a few moments in silence, each man contemplating the beautiful Miss Parker. Preston knew it would be dangerous to spend too much time with her. He would get ideas of how to show her the ways of Blessing which were not like where she came from.

"New York City," Preston said. "Why there? We had a chance if she'd come from someplace western, but the Big Apple is not exactly for girls who live a country life."

"That's the damn truth," Colby said. He got up and glanced out the window. "She's in the bedroom. All curled up in that big bed. She's got to be lonely there."

That bed was perfect. Large enough for the three of them. It was best he put that right out of his mind. No sense in dwelling on something that would never happen with a New York City girl.

Preston glanced at his friend. In the last two years, he'd seen so many good changes in the man. When he first came to work for the Parkers, Preston hadn't trusted him. A man from prison with nothing and nowhere to go. A desperate man trying to start fresh.

But now, he'd filled out, learned some skills, and even settled into the ranching life. If they lost these jobs, Preston wasn't certain what would happen to Colby.

Preston could go to work for his family. But Colby could not return to Louisiana where everything went wrong for him.

"No matter what happens, we've got to stick together," he told his friend, the man he considered a brother now.

"Agreed." Colby ran his finger through his dark brown hair. Preston thought he needed a trim around the ears, though. With his neat mustache and beard, he looked like a man from the 70s. He wasn't sure if their new owner would go for that.

When he studied Colby, he noted the rough lines in his forehead and the biceps that looked like he was training to be a wrestler. The large hands, the dark eyes, and the sharpness of his tongue let you know he didn't mess around.

There was an edge to him that Preston never wanted to cross and a wariness about him that didn't let him get close to people.

But today was the first time he'd been interested in a woman and now she was here. What the hell did they do with that?

Nathan, the Parker's lawyer had been quiet about the details of the will. Especially considering the ranch. Their futures were up in the air.

The memory of Jim White hit him and he groaned.

"Once Jim finds out she's here, he'll be like a magnet sticking to her. We won't be able to get rid of him," Preston said.

"Oh, hell no," Colby said. "Maybe we should tell her about him."

"No," Preston said. "We cannot try to persuade her in any direction about this ranch. We're too close to it. All we can do is show her how beautiful it is and maybe even tell her about the history of the property. After all, this is her heritage."

"True," Colby said. "She acted like her father had never mentioned the land or his parents."

That was definitely odd.

"Who in town knew the Parkers when their son lived here? Is anyone still alive?" Colby asked.

"Yeah," Preston said. "Granny Jones. We'll have to tell Kalie about her. She might be interested in going and talking to her. She might learn why her father and her grandparents never spoke to each other."

With a sigh, Colby glanced at his watch. "As much as I'd like to be over there sharing that big bed with her, I guess it's time for us to bunk down. Ranch work starts early."

Indeed it did. It was long hours but satisfying work.

Colby stood. "I know what I'm going to be dreaming of tonight. The feel of those sweet cheeks snug against my cock in the entryway to the store. Damn, if we'd been alone, it could have gotten pretty wild, very quick."

Preston laughed. "I think you would do better thinking of a nice long, warm shower, where you're jerking off. That's the only relief you're going to get tonight."

"Or tomorrow night, or the one after that," Colby said. "I don't think Miss Priss is into cowboys. Especially ones with a rap sheet."

Colby didn't like to talk much about how or why he'd been convicted. It was a painful subject for him, so Preston didn't bring it up. But the man had turned his life around and Preston considered him as a brother.

"All right, time to go to bed. Lock the doors, so we're protected from Kalie breaking in and taking advantage of us," Preston said.

Laughter came from Colby as he headed toward his room. "Now you're dreaming."

CHAPTER 6

The next morning Preston had gathered the eggs
and fed the chickens while Colby took care of
the horses. Today, their plan was to check on the cattle and
make certain they still had enough grass before moving
them to the next pasture.

As he walked toward the barn, he saw Kalie sitting
outside drinking coffee, gazing out at the land.

This morning she wore jeans and a no-sleeve T-shirt
that clung to her figure. Her dark hair was pulled back in a
ponytail and she looked like she was sixteen, not in her
twenties. Her laptop sat on the table in front of her.

He walked toward her and saw Colby come out of the
barn. The two of them arrived at the table at the same time.

"Good morning," he said. "I gathered the eggs this
morning. Here you go."

Staring at them, she glanced up at him. "Is that poop on
them?"

He laughed. "Yes, ma'am. I like to rinse them off before I put them in the refrigerator."

"Why aren't they white?"

"Because the hens have brown feathers. The eggshell color depends on the breed of the hen and ours have brown feathers. Still the same nutritional value."

Staring at the eggs, she didn't reach for the bucket he'd placed them in.

"The yellow inside will be darker because our hens are free-range. We let them roam around the yard and eat all the bugs they can find."

A shiver went through her.

"Sorry, this city girl is getting an education," she said. "Just don't tell me about the beef and what makes it different. I like a good steak cooked in butter."

Colby grinned.

She threw her hands up. "I can't find the router in the house. And my phone is not picking up out here. Didn't they have internet?"

The two men grinned.

"No, ma'am," Preston said. "Lillian didn't have any need for a computer or a laptop or even an iPad. Believe me, I tried to get them to start putting all the cattle records online and they just looked at me like I was crazy."

Shaking her head, she gazed up at them. "I've got to have internet. Without it, I can't work."

Colby snickered.

"Only way to get internet in this part of the country is with satellite," Colby said.

Staring up the two men, she shook her head.

"Please sit down, gentlemen, staring up at you in the blinding sun is a little much right now. I'm still on New York time and I woke to the sound of the rooster crowing. It wasn't even light outside yet."

They pulled out a chair and sat at the porch table.

"Then I tried to get the internet to work. I tried the television, but there are only two channels. Two. And one I refuse to watch."

A grin spread across Preston's face. She was learning what it was like to live without all the modern contraptions.

"We have satellite television over at the bunkhouse. You're welcome to come watch it."

"You don't have internet?"

"No," Colby said.

"How do you stay in touch with family, friends, business acquaintances?"

The two men shrugged their shoulders. "No need."

"Not even college friends?"

Colby smirked. "Never went to college. Not even in prison."

Her emerald eyes widened. "You went to prison? What for?"

Preston watched as his friend's eyes dipped to the ground. "Escaping. Car theft. Three years in Angola. A hell hole in Louisiana."

Licking her lips, she stared at him and Preston could see she was wary. "What were you escaping from?"

"That is on a need-to-know basis," he said. "Let's just say sometimes there are far greater punishments than those from breaking the law."

It was quiet at the table and Preston could see she was mulling over his comments. "And since you got out?"

"Your grandparents took me in and helped me get a fresh start. I'm forever indebted to them. They were good people."

A sigh escaped between her lips and she shook her head. "Oh, how I wish I'd learned about them sooner. I wonder why they never contacted me."

There was so much she didn't understand and know about their community, and Preston could just bet that her father leaving may have something to do with what went on here. Most of them accepted and thought nothing about it, but occasionally, someone would object and if her father was a prude, then he would want nothing to do with Blessing.

"If you go to town, let us know. We usually try to pick things up at the grocery store whenever someone makes a trip in," Preston told her.

Her brows raised and she gave a little laugh. "I know. I learned that yesterday."

Colby smiled at her. "Small town with very few available women."

"Not my problem," she said, giving him a glare. "No, I think I'll contact someone and get them to install internet and television while I'm here. Surely someone has a short-term plan."

The two men glanced at one another and Preston knew Colby was responding to the words *short-term.*

"What are your plans for the day?" Preston asked.

"We'd like to take you horseback riding around the ranch," Colby said. "Show you the land you now own."

A frown appeared on her face. "I've got to find internet first. Whether that means someone comes out and puts it in the house or I have to go to town. Plus, I've ridden a horse only twice."

They both grinned.

"Well, you know the basics then. We can teach you the rest."

She nodded. "Today, I'd like to spend some time in the house, snooping. Trying to find out more about my grandparents. Get the internet hooked up and rest. Could we go tomorrow?"

"All right," Preston said, thinking he could understand her wanting to learn about her family. "There is a lady in town who is kind of an expert on all the families in this area. Her name is Granny Jones. We thought she would be a good person for you to speak with and learn about your family."

It was all he could do not to say *why your family broke up.*

"Also, my sister is getting married this Saturday night. It would be a good time for you to meet the people in town," he said.

A deep furrow appeared on her forehead. "Oh no, I could not intrude."

"You wouldn't be intruding, you would be getting to know the people in this town. The other families. Maybe someone besides Granny Jones could tell you about your grandparents. Your father. I bet my father went to school with him."

A butterfly darted in the flowers that graced the porch flowerbed and Preston heard a bee nearby, sipping the abundant nectar.

"You're sure your sister wouldn't mind me attending? I mean I'm sure by now her guest list is filled."

He laughed. "Weddings here aren't that formal. The ceremony is outside under the trees and then we're serving barbecue. There will be a rodeo and a dance afterward. By eight o'clock that night, the newlyweds will take off on their honeymoon and the party will continue without them."

Preston wanted her to attend. He wanted her to learn about their ways and the closeness of their community. The way everyone worked together and looked out for one another.

"All right," she said. "It sounds like fun. What should I wear?"

"A nice dress," he told her.

"Are you going?" she asked Colby.

"Wouldn't miss it," he said.

Preston knew Colby couldn't wait to see her reaction to their way of life. And he also planned on riding in the rodeo. The man liked danger. And he'd taken to training wild horses.

"We'll all three go together," Preston said.

"All right," she said.

For a moment, there was silence as she sipped her coffee.

"Well, I guess we better get back to work. We need to go check on the cattle up in the north pasture," he said.

They stood to go.

"Wait, I have another question for you," she said, glancing up at them. "Can you tell me why that bed in the master bedroom is so big? That sucker will sleep four people in it, at least."

Colby snickered and Preston shot him a look.

"You know nothing about Blessing, do you?"

She shrugged. "Not really. My father never mentioned the town to me or my mother."

A grin spread across Colby's face. "You've got to tell her."

"Tell me what?"

As the sun beat down on them, he knew the day was going to be a hot one, but right now, the temperature on the small patio was heating up.

Preston sighed and knew the man was right. "When this town was started, women were scarce and men were tired of being alone. So it became common practice that two men shared a woman. One would be her legal husband, and the second man would be her husband as well, but not in the eyes of the state. That practice continues to this day."

Her emerald eyes widened and her mouth dropped open. "What?"

CHAPTER 7

*C*olby watched as Kalie looked between the two men with shock, her emerald eyes wide with amazement.

"No way. I can understand back a couple hundred years ago why this happened but now? To this day?"

Colby enjoyed the utter look of awe on her face. They had just surprised the woman from New York City and he was reveling in her obvious discomfort.

"Now, it's more of a way of life than a need," Preston said. "In my family, there are two fathers. Both of whom will walk my sister down the aisle. We don't know which man is our real dad; they are both our fathers. I can't imagine living any other way."

Shaking her head, she gasped. "But...aren't there laws against this type of thing?"

"Only one man marries the woman," Preston replied.

When Colby rolled into town and soon learned that

this was a common way of life here, he'd been amazed. And yet after he and Preston shared a woman, he'd adapted immediately. Maybe if there had been two fathers in his household growing up, he wouldn't have gotten into trouble. Maybe someone would have looked out for him.

When he'd first met Preston's family, he'd been jealous. Even when Preston and his brothers argued, there were no fists, no kicking or shoving. Just words spoken with an intensity that soon was resolved and then they were back to being friends.

Even now, Colby had trouble when things got intense. His first line of defense was to punch the hell out of whoever was causing trouble and ask questions later. Preston often was the calming force that kept him out of trouble.

"But how do the men share the woman and why would they accept it? Hell, it's hard enough to find one good man, but now they're searching for two? No way."

Obviously Kalie had not had good experiences with men.

"Very simple," Colby said, leaning down toward her. "The women like it and the men do too."

"But at the same time? How?"

At her question, Preston couldn't help but smile. "One man takes her pussy and one man takes her ass at the same time. They start slow and work their way toward them both taking her."

Flabbergasted, she stared at them and then suddenly her eyes widened.

"Oh my God, my grandparents?"

"Yes, your grandparents," Colby said.

"Ewww, just ewww," she said.

"No, it's all right. It's a way of life here," Preston said. "When you attend the wedding with us, you'll see. Married threesomes with children running about. It's an accepted way of life."

She jumped up and paced across the patio, her eyes wide, her facial expression intent.

"Oh my, this may be the reason my father left and never returned. He was such a prude. A man who didn't believe in so many things. He attended a religious college. After he graduated, he moved to Connecticut and there he met and married my mother. He never came back to Texas," she said softly.

Colby reached out he took her hand. A zing of awareness spiraled up his arm and straight down to his groin.

"Look, this must be a shock to you," he said.

"Yes," she replied, gazing at him.

"Don't judge. Give it some time and when you see the good people together, happy, living their lives the way they want, you'll understand it's a good thing. Maybe your father was too young to understand, but after I realized how the families here were strong and more fulfilled than any family I'd ever seen, I accepted that this was a good thing."

Preston took her other hand. "All we ask is for you to not make a judgment until you've seen our life."

"How many divorces?"

"Very few," Preston said. "Most men and women are married for life."

She nodded. "Just like my grandparents were married for life. But who was the third man?"

"Ben Jones," Preston said. "We mentioned him last night. He's been dead for over ten years. I believe that Granny Jones was his sister."

Glancing down, Colby realized they both still held her hands.

"Thanks for telling me. It makes me even more curious and I can't wait to speak to Granny Jones about my grandparents and my father. I'm not a prude. I don't know if I could do what this town believes in, but I'm open to learning more about what goes on here before I return to New York."

There it was again, she still planned on returning. Releasing her hand, he glanced down the lane at the sound of a car.

"Jim White," he said. "He's driving up the lane now."

"The man who disliked my grandparents?"

"Yes," Colby hissed, knowing they should let her form her own judgments about the man, but it was so hard.

She watched as the big diesel pickup truck with a gun rack in the back pulled up. Jim stepped out, his jeans had a crisp line down the center of each leg and his shirt was starched and stiff. Just like the man.

"Good morning," he said, walking over to the table with a smile the size of Texas on his face. "I wanted to come and welcome you to Texas."

"Thank you," Kalie said.

"I'm Jim White," he said, holding out his hand. "I'm one of the people offering to buy this property from you, so you can return as quickly as possible to New York."

"Kalie Parker," she said, taking his hand. "Thank you, but I'm kind of taking some time off and learning about my family. No need to get in a hurry."

Colby was so proud of her for not taking his bait.

"Boys, how are you?"

"Doing well, Mr. White," Preston said.

"I'm feeling a mite ornery," Colby said. "I hate to tell you this, but you just stepped in chicken shit."

The man's eyes widened and he scurried to the grass and tried to clean the imagined poop off his boots.

It was all Colby could do to keep from busting out loud. Preston sent him a look that clearly said to behave, but he didn't want to. He wanted to get into trouble.

"If you'll excuse me, I need to go saddle the horses and prepare to check on the cattle," Colby said. He tipped his hat to Kalie. "Ma'am, we'll talk more later."

She nodded.

"I'm going as well," Preston said. "I'll text you the number for the internet company."

"You don't have internet?"

"No," Kalie said.

"Oh, come over to my ranch. We have the high-speed internet and you're welcome to use it."

Colby gave a chuckle. The man knew just how to tempt Kalie.

"This afternoon, I'm busy, but if they don't get mine hooked up soon, I may take advantage of your offer."

The man grinned. "Let's sit down and talk about this property. I'm sure you're ready to sell it and get on back to the big city."

Colby knew he better walk away or he was going to be picking up that store-bought cowboy and putting him back in his big truck. The bigger the truck, the weaker the man.

Preston walked up beside Colby.

"Not a bad way to start the morning," he said.

"No, but I told you Jim would be showing up, and sure enough, here he is."

"I'm hoping he'll stick his size seven boot in his mouth and she'll tell him to crawl back in his monster truck and go home," Preston said.

"Let's hope. You know, I really did like the way you explained our little town to her. Shame she won't stay and experience our way of life."

Preston grinned. "One step at a time, brother. One step at a time."

CHAPTER 8

*T*he next day, Kalie called her friend Stacy.

"You are not going to believe what I learned yesterday," she said.

"Your father's family are aliens?" her friend spouted off. "And that's why he never told you about them."

Kalie laughed. This was what she loved about the woman. Her irreverent sense of humor often made Kalie feel better about whatever was going on in her life.

It was the reason they were such close friends.

Plopping into a soft chair, she glanced about the house. "The place is a small mansion that needs some updates, but it's a really nice home. But the biggest piece of news is that this town and my grandparents believe in two men with one woman."

"Shut the fuck up," she said into the phone. "No way. Your grandparents? Ewww…old people sex."

Laughing, Kalie still found it hard to believe herself.

"Well, their partner died ten years ago and it had only been my grandfather Will and grandmother Lillian for the last ten years. But I'm wondering if this is why my father never told me about them."

Her father had been very old school when it came to what happened in the bedroom or between a man and woman. No premarital sex. She could count on one hand the number of times she'd witnessed her parents kissing.

"Are you certain that Grandpa Will was really your grandfather? Maybe the other man was your father's sperm donor. And with two men, why didn't they have more children? You would think you would have a whole passel of cousins somewhere."

It was a legitimate question, but she wasn't certain she would ever learn the answer since they were both gone.

"There's a woman in town that I plan on seeing who Preston and Colby think could tell me why my father left and never returned."

There was a moment of silence. "And who are Preston and Colby?"

Laughter bubbled up from Kalie. "Two very handsome cowboys who wear their Levi's tight, and look really hot with their boots and cowboy hats. They work the ranch. At least until I sell the place."

The memory of Jim White coming to visit her yesterday made her cringe. The man had been obnoxious and so full of himself that she'd almost puked within the first twenty seconds of meeting him. Sanctimonious as hell. His offer would be the last she would consider.

"Hmm…you're at your grandparents' ranch where they were in a menage relationship and the whole town believes in two men for every woman? Girl, you have landed in paradise. Why the hell would you want to come back here?"

Just like Stacy to think this was a good thing. Kalie just felt so unsure. It was so odd and she knew nothing about how it would work with two men, but she was curious.

"Why haven't you grabbed those two hunky cowboys and tried out this new arrangement?"

That was easy.

"Because they're my employees and one of them hit on me in the grocery store before he learned I was his boss. The man wanted to pour cold beer over my naked body and lap it up," she said, the thought still sending tingles of awareness down her body.

On a hot summer day, that cold beer would feel really good.

Stacy laughed. "You were complaining about the lack of men here in New York City who like their sex a little rough and the universe delivered, and you said no?"

It was true. But she was so uncertain, and she didn't like not knowing what she was getting into.

"Honey, what are you thinking? Did that plane ride kill off some brain cells? You're a very smart woman. Try it out. For goodness' sake, you're in the right place to test the waters and find out if this would be something you'd be interested in. These men can give you the rough sex you desire," she said.

Just then a knock sounded at the door. She glanced out the window and saw the truck from the company going to install her connection to the world.

"Gotta go, the internet guy is here and I need it set up so I can get some work done."

"Tonight, why don't you find yourself some porn that involves two men and one woman. Maybe that would answer your questions."

That wasn't a bad idea. But would the company be shocked that instead of watching a romcom, she was indulging in porn? Who cares, it was her dime.

"Good idea. I may just do that," she said. "Talk to you soon."

Disconnecting the call, she went to the door. Two hours later, the technician had her set up for satellite internet. Not as great as she had at home, but at least now she could get some work done.

And she could hardly wait to try out the internet tonight.

After dinner, she cleaned the kitchen. She'd gotten caught up on her most pressing work and now she was going to relax and enjoy a movie. One that was the perfect example of two men and one woman.

Ninety minutes later, she shut off the television. Oh my goodness. Her body was tingling in places she'd forgotten about. That movie had been very explicit and she'd seen exactly what happened.

Without thinking, she picked up her cell phone and dialed Colby's number.

"Is everything okay?" he asked.

"No, it's not. Can you and Preston come over here?"

"We'll be right there," he said.

Now what did she do? She'd just invited her employees over with the express purpose of seducing them and she had no idea how to begin.

An idea quickly formed.

She turned the movie back on and fast-forwarded to the section where the two men were taking the woman. The moans and groans reverberated through the living area.

"Grandmother, I'm sorry, if you can see or hear this," she said out loud. "But it's because of you that I'm curious."

A rapid knock landed on the door and she took a deep breath and released it slowly. It had been two years since she'd had sex. Since that time, the men she'd dated had never made it past the first kiss.

If you didn't know how to kiss, you certainly wouldn't be good in the bedroom was her philosophy.

Opening the door, she wished she'd taken the time to put on something sexy or at least brushed her teeth.

"Come in," she said nervous as hell, but knowing this was what she wanted and she needed it now.

Just then a loud moan came from the television and Colby's eyes widened.

"What the hell?" he said as he stepped into the room, glancing at the television.

Preston followed behind him. "What's wrong? Are you all right?"

"No, I'm not all right," she began. "I was curious as to how it is between two men and a woman, so I rented this movie."

A grin spread across Colby's face. "What do you want, darling?"

Maybe it was time to ask for what she wanted. Stop hedging around and just come out with it.

Preston closed the door and leaned against it, staring at her with those dark sapphire eyes, murky with desire.

"I want...I want you to kiss me."

Colby shook his head. "No. I'm not kissing you, because if I start, I won't stop."

"Maybe I don't want you to stop," she said. "But I have this theory that if a man is not a good kisser, he won't be any good in bed."

Preston stepped up and pulled her around to face him. "I'm damn good in bed. And I'm a great kisser."

"Prove it," she said.

Layering his lips over hers, his mouth commanded that she open hers and his tongue swept inside while his hand pulled her face to where she could not resist. In his grasp, he melded her body to his as his mouth worked its magic on her lips. When he released her, she stared at him and touched her swollen lips.

Dear God, the man's kiss was wonderful. A flood of desire rushed through her body and her breathing was rapid.

"My turn," Colby said.

His kiss was different, but just as powerful as he

worked her mouth over and even bit her bottom lip while his fingers held her face in a tight grip. When he finished, she felt like she was on fire. Like a match had been lit and gasoline scorched the earth around her.

"And?" Preston said.

"You know how to kiss, now you need to show me you know how to fuck," she said, hoping for the first time in two years, she was finally going to have great sex.

They surrounded her and her breath quickened.

"God, woman, I can't wait to fuck you," Colby said, pulling her buttocks snug against his cock. "I wanted you the first moment I laid eyes on you in the parking lot."

She swallowed. The words were coarse, yet they also thrilled her.

Nervous, she stood between them, sandwiched and she couldn't help but wonder if this was what it would feel like with two men.

Colby stepped in front of her beside Preston.

"First some ground rules," he said.

Why would they need ground rules?

"I like my sex a little rough. If you can't take that, speak up now."

A thrill went through her straight to her core. Wasn't this exactly what she wanted?

"I haven't found a man yet, who can give it to me rough enough. What do you like?"

"I'm going to paddle your ass and enjoy every moment," he said, gazing at her, his dark brown eyes filled with a heat that seared her and left her wet between her legs.

In the background, the movie played on, the moans of the woman becoming louder.

"And I'm going to want you to suck my cock," Preston said.

She licked her lips in anticipation.

"Will you pour beer over my body?"

Colby grinned. "Gladly, honey."

"Will you take me in my ass?"

How long had she been dreaming of someone taking her in her backside?

"Not tonight," Preston said. "But we will put a butt plug in there to start preparing you. We don't want to hurt you."

She glanced up at the television. "That woman didn't need preparation."

"She's a porn star. You're an anal virgin. Believe me, we can't wait to take you there. Both of us at the same time, but you're not ready for our big cocks."

Staring at them, she felt her body responding to their stares. Tonight, they would make her theirs in every sense of the word.

"I like to tie women up," Preston said. "Are you agreeable?"

Her breath caught in her throat. It really was like the universe delivered to her exactly what she wanted.

"Absolutely," she said, her breathing coming more rapidly.

"So you're agreeable to spankings, being tied up, and anal sex. Anything else you want?" Colby asked.

"Yes," she said. "Nipple clamps. I've always wanted to try them."

The two men grinned at each other.

"One other thing," Preston said, "when we tell you to strip, we'll expect you to drop your clothes no matter where we are. We'll take you whenever, wherever we want. Also, we may tell you to remain naked all day long."

She licked her lips. "If I have to get on a conference call, I'll have to put my clothes on."

"That's all right, but just as soon as you hang up, you get naked again," Colby said.

"Anything else?" Preston asked. "Anything you don't want to do?"

"Can it just be the two of you and no one else? And you won't hurt me, will you? No hitting me in the face."

"Darling, we're not going to share you with anyone. We're going to make you ours until you tell us to leave you alone. And no, we will never harm you. But we will make you scream with passion."

Heat flooded her womanly parts and a grin spread across her face.

"When do we start?"

"Right now," Colby said. "My dick has been hard with wanting you since the grocery store."

She liked the fact that she made him hard with desire for her. The man was dangerous, on edge, and she liked that about him.

"Strip," Colby commanded.

Biting her lips, she began to unbutton the blouse she

had on. Taking her time, she slowly unwrapped her body while they watched. She liked the way they stared at her. In the background, the woman reached her climax and she screamed. "Fuck me."

The shirt slid to the floor and she worked on the button to her jeans. Once she slid the zipper down, she pushed the jeans to the floor. Only wearing socks, she reached down and peeled them off.

Standing before them in her bra and thong panties, Colby moaned. "More."

Reaching back behind her, she unclasped her bra and let the straps slide down her arms until it fell to the floor.

"Now your panties," Preston said.

Sliding her thong down, she stepped out of the silk and stood before them naked.

"Dear God," Preston said. "I can't wait to fuck you."

Colby stepped up to her and tossed her over his shoulders.

"Time to get serious," he said as he hauled her up the stairs to the second floor.

Bouncing on his shoulder as they made their way to the bedroom, she began to have doubts. What was she doing? Was she crazy?

His fingers moved between her legs and he stroked her clit and she gasped.

"She's soaking," he told Preston.

"Has anyone ever trained you in what they like?"

That was an odd statement. Trained her for what?

"I don't know what you mean," she said.

After they dashed into the bedroom, he slid her down the front of his body. "Good. We'll be the first."

"Get on the bed, on your knees, with your head resting on your folded arms. Stick your ass in the air," Preston told her, walking up behind her.

Colby leaned back and gave her one of those dark stares that sent ripples of anticipation through her. "Tonight, we're going to start training you."

"For what?"

Preston grinned. "In the ways we liked to be pleasured."

Colby slapped her on her naked ass. "Now get moving. On the bed."

The feel of his palm on her ass wasn't bad. It stung just a little and she hurried to do his bidding. Why did she get the feeling that if she disobeyed, it would hurt more?

Getting into the position they wanted, she heard them removing their clothing and she was curious. She wanted to see their bodies and their cocks. She wanted to know what she was getting herself into.

"Head on your arms," Preston said. "Stop looking. You just earned your first punishment."

Colby climbed up on the bed first. "When we're in the bedroom, you will remove your clothes and be naked and ready for us. You will obey us at all times or you'll feel the palm of my hand on your ass. And, darling, nothing would please me more."

She'd had other lovers, but none as demanding as these men, and yet this was what she wanted. This was what she'd been looking for and never found.

Pulling her down to the bed, Colby laid her over his lap. "Tonight, your first punishment is only two licks. Two hard pats that are going to give me so much pleasure. But afterward, I'll make it up to you. The lesson here is to obey. If you don't obey us, you'll get punished."

All she'd done was try to peek and see their bodies. What was so wrong with that?

With his palm, he massaged her buttocks, and she knew that any moment now, his hand was coming down hard.

"Count," he said.

Smack!

This one was much harder and stung.

"One," she cried.

Smack!

This one he made even harder and a heat spread through her buttocks.

"Two," she said with a moan.

Suddenly his fingers were between her legs as he stroked her clit and she ground her mound against his hand.

"We can hardly wait to get inside you. Our cocks are about to explode, so if we go too fast, tell us to slow down. If you're not begging us to take you, then we haven't done our job," Preston told her.

Confusion swirled inside her brain. They wanted her to beg them to take her? Never. She had never begged anyone to fuck her, and they would have to be the most magnificent lovers for her to beg.

Pulling her head toward him, Preston's lips covered

hers and Colby continued his assault on her senses as his tongue trailed all the way down her spine, reaching her crack. Then he pulled apart her buttocks and blew on that most private of spots, sending a swirl of sensations through her all the way to her clit.

"Colby," she gasped, breaking the kiss with Preston.

They placed her on the bed with Preston at her head and Colby by her feet. What was he doing?

Then he spread her legs and looked at her in the most intimate of places.

"Oh, Preston, she's got a gorgeous pussy. And I'm going to taste it."

Anticipation filled her as he spread her folds and placed his mouth on her center, his tongue twirling around her clit. Shockwaves of pleasure pulsed through her and she gripped the sheets.

"We're going to taste you in every way. And if we do it right, you're going to scream with pleasure."

A whimper escaped her as Preston placed his mouth on her nipples, sucking them into his mouth and nipping at the hard pebbles. A pressure built inside her. A pressure she'd not experienced in the last two years, except from her own hand. And this was a hundred times better.

She felt decadent with her legs spread, giving Colby even more access so he could continue giving her pleasure. His tongue lapped at her inner lips and the need to raise her hips and meet him overwhelmed her.

Desire as hot as melted butter coursed through her and she moaned.

Colby's tongue continued to lick her clit, and his finger probed her back entrance. Shock filled her and she tensed, suddenly afraid.

"No, not yet," she cried as she gasped for breath.

Slap! His hand found her pussy and he slapped it hard enough to send a rush of the strangest heat through her. She clutched the sheets of the bed. What was happening?

Slap!

"Don't tell us what to do in the bedroom. You wanted this, and in time, you'll experience more than my finger in your ass."

His fingers toyed with her clit and a hot, slick sheen of her essence coated his digits.

"I think she likes having her pussy spanked," Colby said.

"Do it again," Preston said, rising from her breasts.

Slap!

Suddenly the world exploded around her and she clinched Colby's fingers as he slid them inside her and she screamed her pleasure, the sound echoing in the room. Where did that come from?

"That's it, honey," Preston said. "Come for us."

With a sigh, she let the world right itself as she came down from the high and gasped as Colby lay on the bed on the other side of her. Once again, she was sandwiched between them and she liked the feel of their big hard bodies surrounding hers.

"Did you like it when I spanked your pussy?" Colby asked.

What was she supposed to say? It seemed so unnatural

when his finger rubbed her ass, and yet when he spanked her pussy, a rush of heat consumed her.

"Answer Colby, Kalie. You must be honest with us. We want to give you everything you like. We want to know what excites you."

With a sigh, she quietly said, "Yes, it felt strangely wonderful."

They pulled her into an embrace between them.

Preston rolled onto his back and Colby lifted her and placed the entrance to her pussy on top of his cock.

"Preston…" she said. "Make it really good."

"Darling, you're going to love my cock filling you. I'm going to shove it so far in, you're going to think it's coming out your throat. But more than anything, I'm going to make you scream when you come."

Rising just a little, Preston kissed her again on the lips, nibbling at her bottom lip. Heat swirled inside her once again.

Breaking the kiss, Preston smiled at her, his fingers tweaking her clit, sending passion flowing through her.

With Colby's help, she sank lower onto his cock, stretching and filling her.

"Oh, more," she groaned. "So big and tight. Give me more."

As she rose and slid down his cock, the friction between them heated and she moaned as her pussy clenched around his cock. Pleasure had her moaning, her breathing rapid and fast.

His hands were on her breasts as he tugged and pinched

her nipples, spreading hot lava through her limbs. With a moan, she closed her eyes and let her head roll back.

"Open your eyes, Kalie. I want to see the passion in your gaze. I want to stare at you when you come."

Once again, she opened her eyes, her breathing harsh, and then Colby rubbed his finger at her back entrance. She tried not to panic as he slid his finger into her ass, swirling it around. A burst of desire exploded inside her like a bomb and she leaned back toward Colby.

How could something so depraved feel so good? She'd never imagined a man's finger bringing her so much pleasure.

"Don't come," Preston said.

How was she supposed to stop the rush of heat filling her, flooding her, and making her want to desperately find release?

"Hold on," he said. "I'm almost there."

She groaned and it was all she could do not to scream with frustration.

"Now," Preston said.

It was then that Colby's hand landed on her ass, his finger buried deep inside her and she screamed as her body convulsed. Panting, she never imagined what Preston said would be true. That she would loudly proclaim her pleasure. That the feel of Colby's hand landing on her ass would send her over the edge, falling into that blissful oblivion.

Pumping inside her, Preston stared into her eyes as they both reached their climax.

Drained, she slumped onto Preston's strong chest. Was this all? Sure, she'd come twice, but she'd expected more from two men. She'd imagined it even rougher.

When her breathing slowed, Colby lifted her head up off Preston's chest by her hair. "My turn, Kalie. I can't wait to come inside your pussy. I can't wait to make you scream my name."

How could she endure anymore? How could she take another round? And yet her body was already awakening. She wanted to taunt him. She wanted to see just how rough he could be.

"Too late, Colby. I'm done for the night," she said.

His eyes darkened and he yanked her up.

"Oh no, you're not. Watching you fuck Preston, I'm rock hard and ready to explode. This is going to be hard and fast. Can you keep up?"

"I can outlast you," she groaned.

He rolled her onto her back and pulled her to the edge of the bed. Then he lined up his cock with her pussy. He slid inside her, gripping her hips and lifting her to meet him.

Suddenly he grabbed her legs and spread her wide, opening her to his cock. In amazement, she watched as his cock slid in and out of her pussy. Once again, the pressure was mounting inside her and she clenched his cock.

"Give it to me, harder," she moaned.

Once again her body responded, her muscles constricting around and gripping him.

"Baby, you earned yourself another spanking. I'm going

to paddle that beautiful ass of yours until you can't sit down. And then I'm going to put a butt plug in your ass to prepare you for when we both take you. My seed is racing to explode."

Preston chuckled and leaned down and kissed her on the lips. The feel of his mouth on hers, the way his tongue glided over her lips and slipped between them, sent fire racing through her.

Gripping the sheets, she could feel another orgasm building within her. She lifted her hips to meet his thrusts wanting as much of him as she could take. Tonight had been better than she'd ever expected. Better than she thought was possible and she wasn't ready for it to end. Even after both men took her, she wanted more.

Each man felt different. Each man's cock gave her pleasure.

"I'm going to come," she gasped between breaths, knowing she couldn't hold back much longer.

"Not until I say you can," he said as he reached down and slapped her on the ass. The sting warmed her, but also took the edge off.

"Don't even think we're through for the night. I plan on taking you at least twice more before we're done. I want to hear you beg me to let you come."

"No," she gasped.

"Beg, Kalie," he said as his fingers toyed with her clit.

The heat, the pressure, everything inside her was ready to explode all because of this man.

"You're not coming until you beg me," he said. "And I'm about to explode all over you."

"Please," she finally groaned, "let me come."

"More, baby, tell me more."

"Colby, please I need to come," she screamed, not able to hold back much longer.

"Let's see," Colby said, delaying her need. She watched his face and knew he couldn't hold out. One big squeeze and he groaned. "Come now."

This time the explosion raced through her, sending her spiraling out of control. Screaming, she grabbed the sheets to hold on while Preston held her in his arms, rocking her. Colby stared into her eyes and she felt like they were connected.

In his gaze, she saw passion and desire as he came, and that intrigued her.

With a grunt, he pulled out and came all over her stomach.

When he finished, he grinned at her.

"Give me a few minutes and then I'm going to the house and get our toys."

"Toys?"

"Yes, a butt plug and some nipple clamps. We're not done tonight," he said, leaning back against the bed.

CHAPTER 9

$\mathcal{C}$olby woke early the next morning and smiled at the memories they'd made last night. Kalie had been everything and more, and she'd accepted the way he liked his sex rough.

His fingers reached for her clit and he began to tweak the little nub. In her sleep, she moaned and he pulled her toward him.

His penis slid into her wet pussy just as her eyes opened.

"It's not light outside," she moaned.

A chuckle came from Colby. "Ranch work starts early. Fucking starts earlier."

Preston rolled over and pulled her nipple into his mouth. "Starting the day off between your legs is exactly where we're meant to be."

"Guys, it's only been a couple of hours."

Lifting her legs, Colby smacked her on the ass. "Quit

COME HOME TO THE COWBOYS

complaining or you're going to regret it."

Kalie lay on her side with Colby holding her leg up as his cock shoved into her pussy.

Preston rose onto his knees until his cock was even with her mouth. He laid his cock on her lips. "Good morning, Kalie. I'm so damn eager for you to suck me."

With passion-filled sparkling-emerald eyes, she opened her mouth and pulled his member between her lips. She ran her tongue around the bulbous head and he groaned.

Reaching for her hair, Preston pulled her head toward his cock and pressed his member deep into her throat. Then he rhythmically fucked her mouth.

She did not protest, but a moan resounded in the room. Soon, Colby wanted to feel her lips surrounding his cock, sucking on him, but for now, he was enjoying her pussy.

Colby slapped her on the ass and she moaned around Preston's cock.

"Do that again," Preston commanded, his head thrown back.

Placing his palm on her buttocks, he felt her tremble just as his hand connected with the other cheek. She gazed at Colby with lustful eyes as she groaned, the sensation vibrating around Preston's cock.

As long as Colby didn't give her his heart, they were good. However long she planned on being here, he needed to remember it was only fucking, nothing else.

"I'm going to come," Preston told her between gritted teeth. "Swallow it all."

Colby watched as he plunged one last time into her

mouth as he slammed into her pussy. The three of them came together and Colby couldn't remember when he'd enjoyed a woman more.

Kalie would've been perfect if he wanted a wife, but he didn't.

Colby slumped onto the bed and Preston rolled over, his cock limp.

"What a great way to start the morning," Colby said.

Kalie was quiet. Tears streamed down her cheeks and Colby felt his chest tighten. A crying woman was unnerving.

"Why are you crying?"

"I'm sorry," she gasped. "Last night was the best sex I've ever experienced."

"Darling, you need to be finding better partners," Preston said with a laugh. "Or better yet, just stay here and we'll satisfy you every night."

A puzzled look crossed her face, the light from the rising sun filling the room.

Colby rolled over and pulled her in his arms. If she was looking for marriage, he wasn't a man who would ever agree to being together forever. He didn't believe in forever or happily ever afters. The closest he'd come to experiencing happiness was with Preston's family.

But once the doors were closed, were they as happy as they appeared?

"Last night, and even this morning, has been special," she said. "It's been two very long years since I've had this kind of sex."

What she didn't know was that there was so much more Colby wanted to show her. Yes, she wanted her sex rough, but he'd learned a long time ago it was better to go slow and build up to the place he wanted to take her.

She reached out and caressed the side of Colby's face and she turned to Preston and stroked his fuzzy face. "Thank you. You've made me very happy."

"Oh, darling, don't think we're done with you," Preston said. "By the time you get ready to go home, we're going to spoil you for any other man. Those city boys back in New York don't stand a chance."

She giggled.

"They weren't doing a good job before."

Guilt twisted inside Colby. Whenever she left, she would never be the same. He'd make damn sure of that.

Preston rolled off the bed.

Time to get everyone moving. Colby wanted breakfast before they began the day and they still had some things for Kalie.

Colby swung his legs over the side of the mattress. "Time to get to work. But first, we need to prepare Kalie."

"Prepare me for what?"

"Honey, eventually, we're both going to take you at the same time and we don't want it to be painful."

"Oh, this is where you introduce me to butt plugs," she said.

Reaching inside the bag he'd brought back from the bunkhouse, he pulled out the box that held their supply of butt plugs.

Taking out a tin of salve, he greased the plastic dowel.

"Up on your knees, Kalie," Colby said, knowing he was going to enjoy doing this. He liked making a woman come, especially if it was a little painful. No, he never wanted to hurt someone, but a little extra sensation would bring them both pleasure.

Glancing up at him, she eyed the object in his hand and her eyes widened. "That's what you're going to put inside me?"

"Yes," he said. "Now, do what I told you."

"All right," she said, rolling over and getting up on her knees.

"Head down on your arms so your ass is sticking way up. I love gazing at your ass. And I enjoy even more putting something in there. Soon it will be me and Preston."

In the morning light, Preston watched for a moment and then fondled her nipples. Then his lips kissed the side of her neck.

"I'm getting hard watching you on your knees about to take your first plug. Soon, very soon, I'm going to put my cock in your ass and I can't wait," Colby said as his hands ran over her chest and down until he found her clit.

He gave it a twist and she moaned. "Colby."

This was the part he enjoyed as he stepped behind her. With his fingers, he spread the ointment around her little rosebud and then he plunged a finger into her very tight hole.

"Oh," she cried and a second finger joined the first. He twirled his digits around inside her, thinking of the day they both claimed her at the same time. Just thinking about it made him hard again.

He placed the butt plug at her back entrance and gently pushed it in while Preston's fingers tweaked her clit, rubbing the little nub.

"Can I come?"

"Not yet," Colby said as he pushed the dowel in farther. They were almost there, but he wanted her to hold off just a little longer. Reaching down, he grabbed his cock and put it at the entrance to her pussy.

Preston moved his fingers to her nipples and when Colby saw him twist one, he shoved his cock into her pussy.

For a moment, he took the time to enjoy the slide in and out of her tight pussy with his cock. The way she gripped him while Preston pinched her nipples was delicious.

"Darling, I think you should consider getting your nipples pierced," Preston said. "I'd love to tug on the rings. Maybe even your clit."

Kalie gasped as he drove his cock deeper into her. From the expression on her face and the way she gripped his penis, he knew she was close to coming.

With a push, he drove the butt plug all the way in and she screamed.

"Colby," she cried.

The dowel was completely in and he slapped her on the ass. "Now you may come."

She screamed her pleasure and her body shook as

desire rippled through her and onto his cock. It was all he needed to come, and with a final plunge, he coated her pussy walls with his seed.

They collapsed onto the bed and he lay on top of her. "Can you feel the plug inside you?"

"Yes," she gasped.

"Every few days, we'll increase the size. Soon, you'll be ready for both of us at the same time."

A moan came from her and she rolled onto her back. "Preston, Colby, while I'm here, please wake me like this every morning and put me to bed each night."

"Our pleasure," Colby said, leaning down to kiss her.

"One more thing," Preston said. "You're going to wear this all day and nothing else."

"And you never know when we'll come in to check on you," Colby said. "If you're dressed, you'll be punished."

Oh, how Colby wished she would disobey. Last night, he'd been fairly gentle with her, but he couldn't wait to give her a real taste of what he longed to do to her.

CHAPTER 10

*P*reston tied his bolero tie and pulled on his western jacket. Yeah, it was going to be a hot day in Texas with sweltering heat, but this was his sister's wedding and he wanted to look nice. Plus, he wanted Kalie to think he looked good.

"We're getting too attached," Colby said.

For two days now, they had been fucking her like crazy and they were both loving every moment.

Yes, it was true, but he was not going to tell his friend that. If he could share a woman with anyone, it would be Colby, but the man had hurts that had not healed from his time spent in prison. Unfortunately, Colby never intended to marry.

Right now, if Kalie would say yes, Preston was ready to get down on one knee and propose. The woman was perfect for him and his lifestyle, and today, he would learn how his family accepted her. If she fit in, then he was ready.

But Colby was not. And he didn't know how to get him there.

"I know you don't ever want to marry. But have you ever thought that your marriage would be different than your parents'?"

Turning, Preston glanced at his friend wearing a very stylish jacket and matching hat. He also carried a bag containing his rodeo clothes.

"They say that your marriage will be like your parents. My father beat the shit out of my mother and me. Until, finally, she got wise enough to leave him. Then she married another man who not only beat both of us, but he liked to take cigarettes and put them out on me." Colby sighed. "And my damn teachers were too afraid of him to say anything."

Preston had known of some of this, but not all of it.

"Why did you steal the car? You've never told me about what drove you to take someone's car and run."

Shaking his head, Colby turned away. "Let's make today a good day. Let's have fun and enjoy your sister's wedding. Then, tonight, we'll come home and fuck Kalie. But if I tell you what happened and why, it will ruin the day. I don't want to do that."

That was fair. And it was Colby's decision on when to tell him what happened. He'd waited two years, he could wait a little longer.

"Let's go get Kalie and head to the wedding," Preston told him.

A grin spread across Colby's face. "I bet she looks so damn hot, it's going to be hard not to take her up to the bedroom and do her before we leave."

Preston grinned. "We don't have time. But I know something that will keep us intrigued all day."

They walked out of the bunkhouse and Kalie met them at the front door to the main house, and it was all Preston could do not to carry her up the stairs and strip the clothes from her body.

"Damn, darling," Colby said. "Are you trying to make us miserable all afternoon?"

She laughed.

"It's a wedding," she said.

She wore a flowing dress that came down almost to the floor. It was a summery short sleeve that made her look like a flower bursting with blooms. The dress was fitted, but not tight, and did not hide her curves, but rather accentuated them.

"I'm going to be tempted to pull down your string sleeves and pull out your nipples and suck on one," Colby told her. "In fact..."

"Colby, no," she said with a laugh, knowing he was just about to pull out her breasts.

"Did you tell me, no?"

"Yes," she said. "We don't have time."

"Remove your underwear," Preston said, knowing it

would drive him crazy all afternoon thinking that beneath that dress, she was naked.

"What?" she asked, stunned.

"Remove your underwear," he said again. "I want to think about your sweet pussy all afternoon. I want to know that I can take you to the barn, lift up that dress, and take you right there."

Colby glanced at him and smiled. "Damn, that's good, Preston."

Lifting the dress, she slid down the silk thong underwear and he grabbed them and held them to his nose.

"Aww, that sweet smell that I love so much," he said as he stuffed them into his pocket.

With a gasp, she gazed at him. "Preston."

"Sorry, darling, they are mine now," he said. "Let's go. We need to get there or my mother is not going to be happy with us for being late."

"In the truck," Colby said. "I'm driving."

"But we could take my car," she said.

"No," Preston said. "We want you sitting between us."

It was only a ten-minute drive and he wanted to feel Kalie snug up against him, pressed between him and Colby right where she belonged.

Soon the truck pulled up in front of a large, beautiful two-story home with a wraparound porch.

"Where is the wedding being held?" Kalie asked.

"In the back," he said.

Colby helped her slide out of the truck, her dress riding up past her knees.

"Darling, don't show that beautiful shaved pussy to anyone but me and Preston. I'd hate to have to turn you over my knee right here and paddle that luscious ass of yours."

"Colby," she said blushing. "My dress slides up. You don't have to worry. I'm very self-conscious of the fact that I have no underwear on."

He grinned at her and Preston came up beside her and took her arm.

"Come on, darling. We want to take our seats before the ceremony starts."

When they walked around the back, Preston smiled. The family had been working on expanding the deck so his sister could be married there beneath the awning. The house was edged with blooming perennials and hanging baskets dangled from the eves. On the deck were large candle holders and two big pots of flowers.

His mother and sister had been working hard to get everything prepared.

Music started and they quickly took seats on the bride's side of the folding chairs. Colby went in first, then Kalie, and finally Preston.

The grooms and two groomsmen exited the house and stood beside the preacher.

Kalie leaned over. "She's marrying two men?"

"No, only Michael Thomas, but she's committing herself to both men," he told Kalie. "It's our way. Both are her husbands, but she's only legally married to one."

The wedding march sounded and they all stood and

turned to see his two fathers leading Ashley down the aisle in her white wedding gown. A big smile spread across her face as she looked at her men waiting for her on each side of the preacher.

Yes, he'd seen ceremonies like this most of his life, but this one was really special. This was his baby sister, and while at first, he had been leery of Daniel Hall, he now knew the man had done his best to make certain his family name was cleared of the wrongdoing they had been accused of in the past.

The man raised prize racing horses and he and Michael had become fast friends. Then they started courting his sister and that had taken some getting used to. But, now, here they were on their wedding day.

With mixed emotions, he watched as his fathers handed his sister off to her grooms. It was hard to let her go.

The next ten minutes were spent saying the vows and when his sister repeated hers to both men, Kalie appeared astonished.

"She's vowing to both men," she whispered.

He smiled and nodded, feeling emotional. Soon, the three of them would leave on their honeymoon, and it wouldn't be long until his parents had grandchildren and he had nieces and nephews.

Glancing at Colby, he saw the stoic expression on the man's face. If only he would accept that the two of them should marry a woman and share her between them. Especially this woman between them now.

"You may kiss your bride," the preacher said.

Both men turned Ashley into their arms and laid one on her. A rush of warmth filled Preston. He was so happy for Ashley, and he prayed these men would take good care of her or his brothers and fathers would let the men know their feelings.

Ashley took both of her men's arms and they walked out toward the barn.

They were married and an intense feeling of jealousy overwhelmed Preston. Damn, but he wanted to get married, start a family, and share a life with a woman he loved.

His fathers stepped in front of the crowd. "We'd like for everyone to join us in the barn to celebrate the wedding of our daughter. We've got barbecue, a rodeo later this afternoon, and then this evening, a dance. Please stay and enjoy yourselves."

They rose and Preston saw his mother racing toward him. Oh no.

"Incoming," he said softly.

Colby laughed. "You've got plenty to answer for."

"Preston, wait right there," his mother said.

She rushed up to him and then her eyes widened at the sight of Kalie as she looked her over from head to toe.

"Hello," she said. "I'm Elizabeth Nash, Preston's mother."

"Nice to meet you. Kalie Parker," she said, taking his mother's hand.

"Oh, from the Parker family," she said. "I went to school with your father."

"Really," Kalie said.

"Oh yes, the last time I saw him, he was headed off to college," she said. "Shame he's never come back."

There were rumors about Kalie's father, but Preston was not going to speculate. In fact, he hoped to take Kalie to meet with Granny Jones.

"I've got to run, but I wanted to meet you," she said. "Let's chat more later. Right now, I've got to make certain the caterers are prepared for us. And Preston, we could have used your help last night."

Guilt spread through him. What could he say? He had spent the evening between Kalie's thighs and he'd completely forgotten about helping set up the wedding.

"Sorry, Mother," he said. "I was busy."

Her brows rose and she walked away.

Oh, yes, she knew and there would be hell to pay later.

Colby snickered. "You should have been here last night."

"Yeah," he said. "But I was distracted."

He reached down and squeezed Kalie's ass. "God, I can't think at all knowing you're naked beneath that dress."

"Let's go eat," Colby said. "I need to keep up my strength for later."

"What's later?" Kalie asked.

"He's riding in the rodeo," Preston answered.

Kalie turned and placed her hand on Colby's chest. "No. It's too dangerous."

Colby glanced down at her hand and then he gazed at her. "The very reason I love it, darling."

"Don't worry, he's too mean to get hurt," Preston said.

Each man took an elbow and led her toward the barn. Preston watched as Kalie took in the sights and sounds of the wedding. After everyone went through the buffet, they found a table with his long-lost brother Luis.

"We missed you, man," he said as they sat.

His brother who looked a lot like himself, nodded. A Navy SEAL, he was recently honorably discharged from the military. His time away had changed him.

"It's been a tough year," Luis said. "Who is she?"

"Kalie Parker," Preston said. "She's Lillian and Will Parker's granddaughter."

The man nodded. "Sorry to hear they're gone. They were good people."

Luis frowned at Colby. "And who are you?"

"I'm just a guy who works on the Parker's ranch. I came through here on my motorcycle and decided to stay," he said.

"It's a good place," Luis said.

The military had made him even quieter and more reserved, and the muscles on his arms were bigger than many bodybuilders. No wonder he was a retired SEAL.

His sister Jane came to the table. At eighteen years of age, she was just starting to become beautiful, and he worried about her and the boys she was dating.

"Mom wants us to take a group photo," she told Preston and Luis.

"No," Luis said.

"Come on, we don't know when we'll all be together

like this again. Ask Kalie. Her father never came back to Blessing. She didn't even know her grandparents existed."

The man stared at Kalie. "That true?"

"Yes," she replied.

He sat there finishing his lunch. The SEALs stripped his brother of emotions. Preston hoped that while his brother was home, he would regain some of his old self. Right now, he was cold.

Luis took a drink of ice tea, glanced at Kalie, and then back to Preston.

"All right," he said. "Let's make this quick."

Preston glanced at Colby and he nodded. He would watch over Kalie while Preston did his family photos.

As soon as he walked up, his mother took him by the arm. "I like that girl. You two seem quite cozy. Is it serious?"

"Doubtful," he said. "She's here to sell her grandparents' ranch and then she's going back to New York."

His mother frowned. "You're a Nash. Use your charm and convince her to stay."

If only he could.

After they finished with pictures, he went back to the table and his mother followed him. Luis sat and kept glancing between him and Kalie.

"Kalie, I'm so glad you're here today. This is the first time Preston and Colby have brought a girl to a family event. I knew your grandparents and your father. They were such lovely people. That ranch has been in the family for generations. It would be a shame to see it sold off to strangers."

"Mom," Preston warned, "this is Kalie's decision."

"I know, son, but you know how much I hate change," she said. "And you kids are grown and getting married and well…"

Just then his father announced on the speaker. "Let's head out to the arena for the rodeo."

His mother growled. "A damn rodeo at a wedding. I did my best to get rid of that, but your father insisted. Told me if he was paying for the wedding, then he was going to have a rodeo."

Preston laughed. His father had been holding impromptu rodeos for years. Though he no longer participated, he loved to watch them.

"I better go get changed," Colby said. "Don't want to ruin my good clothes."

"Oh, there goes Michael's mother. I need to speak to her," his mother said and hurried away.

Luis stood. "Nice to meet you, Kalie. I'm going to head back to my ranch."

He'd bought the Rocking B Ranch not far from here with his trust fund and had plans to revitalize the place. Preston hoped the hard work would help him get over what happened to him overseas.

They watched as he walked away.

"Quiet," Kalie said.

"Yes, the war really changed him. I hope being around people who love him helps him find himself."

"I can't imagine what he's seen," she said before she whipped around to face him.

Kalie gazed at him, a smile spread across her face. "So you've never brought a woman around the family before?"

"No," he said. "I thought it would be good for you to see how two men can marry the same woman. And I wasn't about to miss today."

"It looks like most of the town has turned out for this wedding," she said.

"Everyone but Jim White's family. We're not good enough for him and his bunch. Never have been and that's quite all right," he said. "Come on, let's get a seat on the bleachers. These events usually don't last long."

An hour later, Preston and Kalie sat waiting for Colby to ride. He leaned over and whispered in her ear.

"He's going to be out of commission tonight," he told her.

She laughed. "If his horse bucks as much as that last one, I can understand why."

Just then they saw Colby sitting in the chute. "Oh no, he's next."

Squeezing his hand, she held on to him tightly. "I don't want him to get hurt."

"No one wants to get hurt," Preston said.

"Why does he do this?" she asked.

"Well, if you haven't noticed by now, Colby is a danger junkie. Hell, he'd ride a tornado if he thought he could live to tell the tale. I think because of his past, he now seeks out danger just to show he can conquer the situation."

As they released the gate, she turned and glanced at him.

"Here he goes," Preston said.

For a moment, they stared in silence as Colby rode the bucking horse bouncing all over the arena, but he held on until his eight seconds were up and he managed to jump off the animal.

The horse snorted and then trotted out of the arena.

Colby walked rather stiff-legged to the gate.

"Colby King is in the lead with eight seconds," Preston's father called.

A few minutes later, Colby reappeared in his dress clothes and sank down gently on the bench beside them.

"You did good," Preston said.

"Scared the crap out of me," Kalie replied. "What do you like about this?"

He grinned at her. "For me, it's all about taming the animal. Showing them who's in control. Just like what I do with you."

A blush spread across her face and Preston laughed.

"But, I will admit, it's just not as much fun anymore," Colby said.

"Why not?"

"I don't know. The thrill of taming the animal is just not there," he said. He glanced at Kalie. "There are other things I'd rather tame. Nothing like a woman's soft flesh beneath my hand."

Preston grinned.

"What if we skipped the dancing and went home,"

Colby said. "I'm not much of a dancer and there's a beautiful woman who's not wearing any underwear and I can't wait to take advantage of her nakedness. If not, I'm going to take her right there in the truck."

Kalie's eyes widened and her breathing quickened. "Are you ready, Preston?"

"Yes, we were here for the wedding and the barbecue and the rodeo. I'm ready to take you home and fuck you senseless," he said, rising.

A grin spread across her face. "Let's go."

Standing, they hurried down the steps of the bleachers and across the yard.

"Kalie Parker?"

A voice called and she turned. Preston's mother darted across the yard to them.

"I know these guys are eager to take you home, but there's someone I'd like you to meet," she said, taking her by the arm. His mom led her across the yard to an older woman who sat in a chair with a walker nearby.

She led her up to the elderly lady with gray hair and black beady eyes. "Granny Jones, this is Lillian and Will's granddaughter. Seth's daughter."

The older woman reached out and pulled her close. She smiled at her.

"You look like your grandmother. God rest her soul. Your father never returned to Blessing and it hurt your grandmother something fierce."

Sitting under a tree, the older woman gazed at her with curiosity.

"No, ma'am, I didn't even know I had grandparents until the lawyer contacted me."

She nodded. "You probably have a lot of questions about your family. You should come see me sometime soon. I'd like to talk to you."

Preston grinned. His mother had taken things into her own hands. Granny Jones had probably been told Kalie was going to sell the property. She'd known the Parkers and knew they wanted the land to stay in the family. It was the reason they had left it to their only granddaughter.

"I'd love to hear what you could tell me about my grandparents," she said. "Yes, if you're not busy on Wednesday, I'll come see you."

The woman laughed. "Honey, I'm at the age that all I do is sit around and wait for death to claim me. You come any time."

"Thank you," Kalie said as the woman released her.

Preston shook his head and smiled at his mother. He knew what she was up to. And he was pleased. She had just given her nod of approval to Kalie.

"We're leaving, Mom," he said.

She nodded and gave him a wink. "Talk to you soon."

The three of them hurried across the grounds. It would be dark soon and they couldn't wait to get back to the house.

CHAPTER 11

*T*he sun shone brightly in the blue Texas sky as they rode through the rolling pastures. The cows chewed grass and gazed at them with suspicious eyes. It was still a couple of months before they rounded up the bovine and sold them off, but for now, they were happy eating the fresh meal.

Kalie sat on a horse well, and today, she even had a pair of cowboy boots on. They were showing her the land she had inherited. After the wedding, Preston wanted to do everything they could to convince her to stay.

Colby knew Preston had marriage in the back of his mind, but Colby had not been raised by a happy couple. He'd gotten out of one bad situation and he was terrified of getting into another one.

You would think that he would have heard from his mother while he was in prison, but for all he knew, she was dead. No letters, no calls, nothing. And after that last night when he'd run, he wasn't about to learn what happened.

She'd been bruised when he left, but not from him – from the asshole she'd married.

Yes, another one.

Glancing at the sky, he pushed the ugly thoughts from his memory. He did his best not to think of them. But when he did, he'd try to evaluate why he felt this desperate need to run.

Now it was Kalie. Damn, the woman was gorgeous, and from the first moment he'd seen her in that grocery store, it had been instant attraction. It was like his body connected with her, and he should have run, but instead he'd pursued her.

And every day, he grew more anxious and trapped.

Only Preston wasn't running. Preston was in full-pursuit mode and he didn't want her to leave, but to stay and run the ranch. Preston wanted them to promise each other forever and have two-point-five kids.

Kalie had been the first woman to make him think about promising forever, but in his case, he had no examples of happily forever after. He'd been raised by people he never wanted to see again. And he had the cigarette scars to prove it, among other things.

"Why don't we stop under that tree up there and have our picnic," Preston said.

Colby nodded. After the wedding, there was so much on his mind. Watching Preston's younger sister get married had reminded him of everything he was missing out on. Sure, he could get married, but what if the marriage became like his parents'? What if the monster inside him unleashed and he turned into his father, or stepfather, or even his mother? What if he did to his children what had happened to him?

No, just no. He could never hurt a child. Never. And yet those genes were in his blood.

They pulled their horses to a halt and Preston ground tethered his animal and then helped Kalie down.

"You did very well," he said. "It may have been years, but you haven't forgotten how to ride."

"Thanks," she said as she reached into her saddlebags and pulled out the blanket.

Swinging his leg over his horse, he watched the sway of her ass and his cock hardened. A groan escaped him and Preston glanced at him.

"Damn, that's a fine ass," he said.

So far, they had not taken her in the backside, but the day was fast approaching, and he could hardly wait.

"Patience, brother," Preston said grinning.

Reaching into his bag, he pulled out his sack with the toys inside. Today, they were going to play outside in the sunshine.

But his patience was missing and he didn't know how much longer he could hold back. In fact, maybe she should start seeing the anger that rode him hard.

"Strip," he said as he walked up to the blanket.

Turning she stared at him. "What?"

"I said strip. Do it now or you're going to get a spanking," he said.

A frown appeared on her face and she sighed.

"Move it. Last warning," he told her.

She began to undress.

Reaching into the bag, he pulled out rope and a large dildo and then he began to remove his clothes. Today, he felt restless, angry, frustrated by life and how much he wanted her. Damn, it was like she'd crawled inside him and pierced his heart with her ways.

It was better to never become attached to anyone. It hurt way too much when they disappointed you. It was better to scare them away and send them running.

Would Kalie run?

When he glanced up, she was naked and she stood before him proudly. Preston was removing his clothes.

"I thought we were going to have a nice picnic," she said.

"We are, but first we're going to play," he told her. "Hold out your wrists."

Licking her lips nervously, she did what he asked and he tied her wrists together. Not too tight, but enough that she couldn't move them.

Then he removed a blindfold and covered her eyes.

This usually made women nervous and they would tell him to stop, but Kalie stood before him. Her nipples became taut and he took out the nipple clamps and pulled out each nipple to attach them.

That drew a moan from her and he stepped in close. "Anytime you want me to stop, just say so."

"No," she gasped. "More. I want more."

Damn, this woman was greedy. It was another thing that drew him to her but he didn't want to be so drawn that he couldn't let go. He had to push her even more.

He took out a flogger and trailed it across her breasts, down her stomach, to her very center.

"Spread your legs," he demanded.

She obeyed and he trailed the ribbons across her center, lingering on her clit. Raising his hand, he popped her with the flogger and she gasped.

Preston took out a butt plug, the next size up. After he had lubed up the plug, he pushed her over and his fingers began to stretch her.

"Oh, darling, this is the last size. Soon we're going to take you at the same time. I can't wait."

A gasp came from her lips and he rubbed her buttocks with his hand as he eased the butt plug inside her.

Colby stepped up to her and took her cheeks in his hand. "Tell me, Kalie. Who you belong to."

"You, Colby and Preston. You're my Texas men," she said.

He didn't like that response. That meant she was still planning on returning to New York and they were just her Texas playthings. And yet what could he offer her? He wasn't into rings and forever afters.

His lips covered hers in a punishing kiss that had his tongue pushing inside her mouth, his lips demanding she surrender. But he wasn't certain who was punishing whom because she opened her mouth and happily accepted him.

If only he was a man who could offer her more. But his past was much too tainted for any woman.

When he released her mouth, he pulled on the nipple clamps and she moaned. At Preston's nod, they laid her on the blanket.

"Don't come," he commanded as he turned on the vibrator and ran it over her clit.

"Aargh," she cried. "Colby."

"Darling, today, I'm going to make you scream so loud, the cows are going to run." He shoved his fingers inside her along with the vibrator. Preston pointed his cock at her mouth and told her to open and take him between her lips.

Kneeling over her, he plunged into her mouth as her moans became louder while he tugged on her nipples.

Seeing she was about to come, Colby backed off and gave her a break, even though he wanted to spank her. He wanted to punish her, though she'd done nothing wrong.

Nothing except make him feel things he promised himself he would never feel. He was beginning to care about her and that scared the hell out of him. It terrified him.

And because of those feelings, he felt the need to push her to her limits. See if she would break beneath his touch. But so far, she'd taken everything from him.

"Kalie, I'm about to come. Swallow it all," Preston said as he threw back his head and pushed one last time.

As he crawled off her, Colby ripped the blindfold from her and gazed into her eyes. "Are you ready to get fucked?"

"Yes," she cried. "Please, Colby."

She was on the edge and so was he. She'd taken everything he'd given her, but could she take the pounding he was about to release?

Lifting her hips, he lined up his cock with her pussy. "Don't come until I say you can."

A moan came from between her lips and she gazed at him, her emerald eyes sparkling with passion.

"Fuck me," she said.

Why was the woman so willing? Why was she everything he'd ever dreamed about, but knew he could not have?

Slamming his cock into her, she squeezed him hard and he gasped knowing he wouldn't last long.

Her hands were still tied and she tried to reach up and touch him, but Preston pressed them above her head.

"No touching, Kalie, today is about your pleasure," Colby said. "I'm going to fuck you into next week."

On his knees, he held her hips high as he pounded her again and again and he could see the telltale signs in her eyes that she was about to come.

"Don't do it," he said deliberately taking her to the edge. Oh, how he wanted her to come, and then he would have a reason to spank her. A reason to pull her over his knee.

"Colby, I can't," she gasped and then her orgasm exploded on his cock and he grinned as he released himself, shoving into her one last time. He'd never experienced sex like this in his life. It was only with Kalie. She'd crawled up inside him and made him come so hard.

Only with her, did he have feelings growing that he didn't want to recognize, that he didn't want to think about.?

Slowly, he let her hips fall back to the blanket as he slouched to the ground beside her. All three lay there as their breathing slowed.

"You did that on purpose," she said. "You wanted me to lose control and come, so you could spank me."

He grinned and rolled over and faced her. "Darling, no one can ever call you dumb. You're right, I did. Why? Because I love spanking that soft sweet ass of yours. And if you'll give me just a moment, I'm going to enjoy paddling you."

With her wrists still tied, she curled up beside him, touching him.

"There are demons in your soul. I don't know what happened to you or who hurt you, but if it gives you pleasure to spank me, then as long as you don't hurt me, I'm happy. In fact, it really turns me on." She rolled back and gazed at Preston. "Both of you together make me very happy. I can't wait until you both take me at the same time."

What the hell? He was supposed to be scaring her away, and instead, the damn woman liked his spankings. She liked the way they treated her and wanted it all.

Terror filled him as he gazed at her. No other woman had ever accepted him like Kalie, and the need to flee filled him. He glanced at Preston, who smiled and nodded.

What was he going to do?

CHAPTER 12

*K*alie had been here ten days. Almost two weeks and already she was dreading her decision. But what could she do? Her job, her life, everything was back in New York City. And yet, this felt like home and that frightened her.

She had settled into the house and was slowly going through all the closets, chests, and anything that might tell her something about her grandparents. So far, she'd found old photos of her father. His baby pictures and mementos of her grandparents' life.

They looked happy as a family. And yet something must have torn them apart.

Today, she was going into town to speak to the lawyer. She had two offers on the place, but she didn't know what she wanted to do. This was her heritage. And every day, it felt like she was meant to be here, but that couldn't be possible.

After she met with the lawyer, she was going to meet with Granny Jones. This was the meeting she was looking forward to, not the one that would force her to make a decision about the ranch.

Walking out the door, she saw Colby and Preston working with a horse out by the barn. Just gazing at them, she became all flushed. Every day, they surprised her and made her feel more and more like she should be here with them.

Yet, nothing had been said about her staying. What if this was just a casual fling for them? But for her, it felt so much deeper. And how in the hell could she ever date again after experiencing the two of them together?

With a sigh, she blew them a kiss and hurried to the car. They knew where she was going and how this meeting could affect their futures as much as her own.

Getting into the rental car, she tried to think of the pros and cons of selling the property versus moving here. She would have to fly back to New York, pack up her apartment, and give them notice she was leaving. Then drive clear across the country with her things or hire a moving van.

She would have to sublet her apartment for six months until her contract was up. Or she could sell the land and walk out of here a very rich woman.

As she drove out the gate, she glanced back at the house. She would never own anything this nice in New York City. She would have to be a billionaire to own such a home.

And could she walk away from Colby and Preston? This had started as an experiment to experience two men at once. Just sex, but her emotions were getting involved. As much as she had tried not to let them get through the barriers to her heart, she cared about them.

Colby had demons he had yet to tell her about, but she hoped before she left, he would open up and tell her why he'd spent three years in prison. Why he pushed her away, and yet, he'd been the one to approach her in the grocery store.

Preston, dear God, the man was everything a woman could want. Handsome, funny, and endearing, and if anyone would ever look out for her and care for her, it would be him. He was the one who would comfort her and make certain she was all right. The man was perfect for what she wanted in a husband.

And he could fuck her into next week.

In fewer than ten days, they had made her theirs in every sense of the word except for a ring around her finger. And she wasn't ready for that, but could she leave them behind and not regret her decision for the rest of her life?

What if this was where she was meant to be?

Pulling up in front of the attorney's office, she glanced down the road. She liked this small town. It was quaint, and most of the world didn't know about this place and she liked that about the little village.

With a sigh, she got out of her car and walked into the office.

"Kalie Parker to see Mr. Alley," she told the receptionist.

"They're waiting for you in the conference room," she replied and led her to a large room in the back.

When she walked in, Nathan Alley along with Jim White and Zachary McCoy, another ranch owner, were waiting for her.

"Miss Parker," Nathan said, rising as the other men rose from the table. "Good to see you, again."

"Hello, gentlemen," she said, coming in and sitting in a chair that Nathan pulled out for her.

He handed her two folders.

"Let's begin," he said. "In the first folder is Zachary McCoy's offer of the ranch. He's offering two million dollars. He will tear down the house and barns and incorporate the land into his own property and run cattle on it."

The thought of someone tearing down that beautiful house made her sad. It was her birthright. Her grandparents had built it with love and the future in mind.

She nodded.

"Your property backs up to mine, so it would just be more acreage for us," the man told her.

Right now, she wasn't going to say anything but just listen to the lawyer.

Jim White smiled at her. "How are you doing?"

Something about the man gave her the willies. It was like he was smooth talking her so he could take her to the cleaners.

Nathan sighed. "The second folder is Mr. White's proposal. He's offering you three million dollars."

"Wow," she said. That was a lot of money. "What do you plan to do with the land?"

He grinned at her and leaned forward. "We're going to create a subdivision. Divide off the land and sell it as mini ranches. The people from San Antonio and Dallas and even Houston are always looking for a place out in the country. With five-acre lots, they can build the house of their dreams and have a small piece of heaven right here in Blessing."

For a moment, she thought about her grandparents. Would that be what they would've wanted?

"What about the house?"

"Oh, that will be torn down along with the barns. The cattle we'll move over to my ranch."

She gazed at each man. "As you know, I have two hands who work the ranch for me. What would you do for them?"

Zachary McCoy gazed at her. "They would be offered jobs at my ranch. I don't really need any more help, but I'd do that as a courtesy for them."

Jim grinned. "I'd give them a nice severance package."

Not really what she wanted to hear.

Why did this not feel right?

She sat there staring at each man. One was a greedy son of a bitch. And Zachary, she didn't think he was a bad man, just someone who would be increasing the size of his own ranch. She couldn't blame him for that, but it still didn't feel right.

"Gentlemen, I know you've been patiently waiting, but

I'm not ready to make a decision today. I've seen your offers, I've heard what you're going to do with the land, but I need more time. My stay here is running short, so I'll let you know my decision no later than tomorrow."

Jim smiled that creepy-ass smile that she'd come to hate so very much. He leaned over and took his offer from her.

"I'm signing it right here and now. All you'll need to do is add your signature and it's a done deal."

Did he think that because he'd signed the paperwork that this would push her toward a decision? It did just the opposite.

"I'm not signing anything today," she repeated.

They all stood, and Jim White raced to her side of the table. "You'll make the right choice. I just know you will."

He tried to hug her and she stepped back. So instead he grabbed her hand and shook it. A sick feeling overcame her.

Zachary lifted his hat from the table. "Good luck, Miss Parker. It must be a really difficult decision."

"Yes, it is," she said. "So many generations and lives were built around this land. I feel blessed to learn about my grandparents."

He nodded. "I'll be waiting for your phone call, Nathan."

The men walked out the door and she turned to Nathan.

"They both offered a lot of money, but I just don't know yet. Something is holding me back and until I know for certain, I'm not choosing."

The man nodded. "Maybe the decision is for you to stay and take over the running of the ranch."

"I've been considering it. But it's such a life change for me. I don't know yet," she said. "Thanks for being patient with me."

"No problem. I loved Lillian and Will and want to do what's right by them."

Picking up her purse, she walked out of the conference room and headed out the door. Jim White stood outside waiting for her.

"How about some lunch," he said.

Oh hell no.

"Thank you, but I'm sorry, I have another appointment I need to get to," she said.

"Oh, well then, I hope to see you again before you leave town."

"Good-bye, Mr. White," she said and quickly got in her car.

Putting the address into the GPS, she pulled out of the parking lot and drove toward Granny Jones, wondering if the woman could tell her about her family.

Preston had offered to go with her today, but she really wanted to speak with the woman alone.

Pulling up in front of a large Victorian home, she gazed at the house from an older time and admired the gabled roof and wide porch.

After getting out of the car, she hurried up the steps.

The woman met her at the door. "Come on in, child. I've been anxious for this day."

"Thank you for speaking to me today," she said.

"Have a seat on the couch," the older woman said, sinking down into a rocker. "I'm not much good these days for standing. These old bones don't hold up too well."

What could she say to that?

"I'm curious about my family. What can you tell me about my grandparents and even my father."

The old woman took a deep breath and shook her head. "Let's start at the beginning."

Leaning back in her rocker, she began to speak.

"Your father was the only child your grandmother Lillian could have. The doctor told her to never get pregnant again, and before she could stop them, her husbands went and got a vasectomy. It broke her heart, but they didn't want her to suffer the way she had when your father was born."

"I guess that guaranteed she would never get pregnant again," Kalie said.

"Yes, and she wasn't happy about it, even though what they had done was with love for her. So she doted on your father. If he was going to be her only child, then she bought that child anything and everything he wanted. He had the best of everything. But there was one problem."

"What?"

"He hated ranch life. Never took to it from the time he was a little boy. And when he went off to college, he learned that our way of life was not good. He started dating a preacher's daughter and she told him in no uncertain terms that she would never condone our way of life. It was sinful."

Thinking back to her father, she realized he was one to raise hell and damnation at every turn of events. The world was coming to an end and she should be prepared. It wasn't a bad thought, it was just so negative that even today, she found it hard to sit in church.

"He didn't marry that girl because his fathers took him out and tried to talk some sense into him. But your father was a rebellious man. College had shown him that we were heathens and he didn't want anything else to do with the town of Blessing or the lives or the families here. Your grandmother was devastated. She loved him so much. For years, I know she sent him cards and letters on his birthday. Anything to bring him back into the fold, even if he didn't want to live our way of life."

"My father was a cold man," Kalie admitted. He could have done something like this.

"When he married your mother, his family was not invited to the wedding," Granny Jones said. "Your grandmother's heart was broken. For years, she didn't know you had been born. And then she contacted your father and said she wanted to meet you, but he refused. No child of his was going to be influenced by their evil ways."

Because of his inability to accept their life, she'd missed out on meeting her grandparents, and for that, she almost hated him at this moment. He'd always been a callous, stiff man who couldn't show love to the people who cared about him. All he'd had to do was tell her she had grandparents who lived a strange life and she would have accepted them.

But now she'd seen the love in this town between the families and the men and women who lived this way and she felt more loved here than she had at home.

"Two days before your grandfather died, she tried to contact your father. She wanted to let him have one last opportunity to speak to his father, but he didn't take her call."

Damn him!

"He turned away his own mother. At that point, she gave up and decided that instead of leaving the ranch to him, she would leave it to you. Though she knew you had a life in New York City, she hoped that maybe you would come visit and make your own decision about the Sweet B Ranch."

With a sigh, she knew. She knew right then what she had to do and a sense of relief overcame her.

"I wish I had met my grandmother and my grandfather. Truly I do," she said. "I loved my father, but he could be a harsh man."

The old woman reached out and took her hand in hers. "You'll do what's right. And in so many ways, you remind me of Lillian. We were best friends for so many years. I miss her to this day."

Tears welled in Kalie's eyes. Thank goodness, she'd come to speak to Granny Jones.

She could see the woman growing tired and she stood. "It's time for me to go but thank you so much for helping me to understand my family. It's given me so much insight and helped me to make my decision."

The older woman stood and hugged her.

"Good luck, Kalie. You're going to make your family proud."

As she hurried out the door and climbed into the car, she knew what she had to do. Picking up the phone, she called Nathan.

"I've made my decision. I'm not selling the ranch. I'm moving to Texas and I'm going to learn how to run a ranch."

The man laughed. "You don't know how happy that makes me. Will and Lillian would be so pleased."

Now how would Colby and Preston take her decision?

CHAPTER 13

*P*reston kept glancing out the barn to the driveway of the house. They were working up in the loft, moving hay.

"She should be back by now," Preston said, wishing that little red rental car would come pulling up in the drive.

"Don't forget she went to see Granny Jones after the meeting with that lawyer."

"Yes, but I don't trust Jim White. If she told him no, he'd do all he could to convince her to change her mind."

Colby threw a bunch of hay out of the open barn loft window.

"If you were offered several million dollars for land that you know nothing about, wouldn't you take it? I know you're keeping your hopes alive she'll change her mind, but I think we should be thinking about packing our bags."

The man was probably right, but Preston was hanging

on to hope that she enjoyed their life together and would want to stay here.

"And you're not hoping she'll change her mind? I see the way you gaze at her, the way you keep trying to push her away by being more and more rough with her. And believe me when I tell you, I will never let you hurt her."

There was more to Colby's story that he hadn't shared, but Preston knew prison had to do things to a man. It must have changed him. He'd been eighteen when he went to the big house.

Colby speared a hay bundle and shoved it to the side. "What in the hell would a woman like Kalie want with a man like me? I'm not good enough for her, so yes, I keep trying to push her away before she hurts me or I hurt her."

Preston grinned. "Hey, you are human after all. Don't you think I'm just as afraid of her leaving me behind when all I want to do is fuck her every day and maybe spend the rest of my life with her? It's too soon, and yet she's the one I can't stop thinking about."

"Me either," Colby said. "Drives me crazy. All day, it's all I can think about."

"And I think she would accept a man like you. Unless you eat little children for breakfast, I don't think there is much she wouldn't welcome. I don't know what happened to you, but I think you should tell her. Then you would know her feelings and you could stop this bad boy act."

"It's not an act," he said.

"The hell it isn't. Somewhere in there is a kind-hearted man who loved Will and Lillian and would've given them anything they needed. I saw how you acted when Lillian told you she was dying. You cried like a baby."

Preston would never forget that night. How she had been trying to comfort them and telling them she was ready to go. She missed her husbands.

"That's because she and Will were the only people who have ever helped me. When I needed help the most, no one came to my aid. And now, I will never need anyone's help ever again. I intend to make certain of that," he said, his face red from the heat.

Shaking his head, Preston gazed at him. "We all need help from time to time. You're going to need help and I hope like hell I'm there for you. I hope my family and even this town will be there for you. We can't go through life without people being by our side. We all have to help one another."

He stabbed his pitchfork into a pile of hay and shoved it aside. The man had been deeply hurt and he understood that, but how could he think he could get by without needing anyone's assistance?

The sound of a car coming up the lane had him glancing out the window.

"She's home," he said. "Don't ask, don't pressure her. If she's made a decision, she'll tell us."

Colby clinched his fist. "You're right about one thing. Blessing is the only place where I've received help, and yeah, I should be grateful, but sometimes the old memories flare back up, and as she calls them, the demons take hold."

"Well, put them on ice and don't push her away," Preston said.

It was a warm day and earlier they had removed their shirts. He watched as Kalie walked into the house, and when she came out, he figured she was searching for them.

"Up here," he called and she smiled and waved her hand.

Climbing up the ladder, she reached the top and he pulled her up into the platform.

"A hayloft," she said grinning. "With two handsome half-naked men on it."

Walking over, she ran her palm down his sweaty chest, sending ripples of desire down him.

"I'm hot," he said, desire filling him from her touch. God, the woman had no idea what she did to him. His dick hardened.

She turned to Colby. "Your muscles are gleaming with sweat."

And she ran her palm down his chest as well. Taking a deep breath, she moaned and began to undo the buttons on her shirt.

"Wait. What are you doing?"

"I'm getting undressed. Touching you has made me wet and I can't wait to feel your cocks inside me."

Preston laughed. "We've created a monster. She can't get enough."

Glancing at him with a wicked smile, she licked her lips.

"No, I can't. What are you waiting for?" she said as she shucked her jeans.

Colby glanced at her. "Damn, Kalie."

Reaching behind her, he grabbed a rope and quickly wrapped it around her wrists.

Then he pulled the rope pulley until she was strung up naked, her breasts pushed out and nipples tight.

"Damn, woman, I think I'm going to have to fuck you," Preston said at the sight of her struggling with her wrists bound. He couldn't shuck his clothes fast enough.

"I dare you," she said.

They moved her between them with Colby in back and Preston in front. He leaned down and took her nipple into his mouth and sucked the orb. A groan escaped her and she pushed her breasts out to him.

"Take me. Make me yours, Preston," she told him and her words just made him harder.

Colby slapped her on the ass. "You have become quite the little tease."

"That's what you do to me," she said.

"Well, let me help you with that," Preston said as his fingers moved over her clit, tweaking the little button, twisting her flesh, and pinching it until she rolled her head back.

Colby was behind her and he kissed her neck as he rubbed his cock along her backside.

"Soon, darling. Soon. I can't wait to take you in your ass."

"When?" she asked moaning. "I'm ready."

"Maybe tonight. But not here, not like this," he told her.

She pouted her lips.

Preston knelt on the floor and raised her pussy until it was at his mouth.

Then he plunged his tongue inside and she groaned.

"Oh, Preston, yes," she said as he licked her clit, nibbling on the nub.

Colby fell to his knees and spread her ass cheeks and began to tongue her little rosebud. She was being sweetly tortured and she screamed at the feel of his tongue on her backside.

"Oh, God, Colby, Preston," she moaned. "Someone fuck me."

"Not yet," Preston said as he worked over her clit. She tried to buck away, but he held her against his mouth while Colby worked her backside.

Finally, when he knew she was close, he shoved his fingers inside her and Colby shoved his digits in her ass and she screamed her release.

"Oh," she cried, her body tensing as the barn filled with the sounds of her passion.

Hanging there, they both stepped back as she trembled, her eyes glazed with passion. It was so good between them, how could she think of leaving them behind?

Colby gave her a little push and she swung toward Preston. He couldn't wait any longer. On the second swing, he grabbed her by her waist and shoved his cock into her pussy and she grasped him with her legs.

"Preston," she cried. "Oh, please."

Holding her still, he pounded her pussy while Colby ran his cock up and down her crack, his fingers pressing inside her ass.

"This is what it's going to be like when we both take you," Colby whispered into her ear. "I'll take you in your ass and Preston will fill your pussy. Then we'll switch."

"Please," she cried. "I can't wait."

"We're going to fuck you so hard that night, you won't be able to walk," Colby said. "I'll spank your ass until it's nice and pink and maybe even use the flogger on you. Preston will have you suck his cock. We're going to use you until you beg us to stop."

Preston realized this was Colby's way of scaring her. Of making her run so he wouldn't have to admit his growing feelings, but it wasn't working.

No, in fact, Kalie seemed to be enjoying every minute. She acted like she wanted more.

His orgasm built deep inside and he wasn't going to last much longer. If at all.

Grabbing her hips, he slammed into her pussy one last time and his seed exploded inside her.

Colby's fingers were deep in her ass and Kalie screamed her orgasm as he rocked them both until he could no longer stay inside her.

With a gasp, he pulled out and leaned against the barn post for support.

"My turn," Colby said. "Only I'm going to do things a little different. I'm not going to let you come."

Kalie's breathing was rapid and shallow as she tried to

recover. "Oh yes, you are. Except that you will punish me for coming."

"Smart girl," he said as he shoved his cock deep in her.

"If I could reach your cock, I would punish you," she said. "I would squeeze your balls until you were begging me to release them."

Eyes wide, Colby laughed. "Our girl is learning."

"I would take the flogger and swat your ass with it and then trail it down your penis until you were begging me to let you fuck me."

Preston stood back, catching his breath and grinning. Kalie had grown a spine and she was letting Colby know that his tactics weren't going to work. He liked the way she stood up to him.

"Then when you came, I'd punish you again," she said. "Two can play this game."

He noticed her words were affecting Colby as his face reddened as he fought to keep from coming.

"Don't come, big boy, or there will be consequences," she purred at him. "If I can't come, neither can you."

It was at that moment that Colby lost control and he shoved his cock deep into Kalie and she purred like a cat as she took him deep within her.

At the last moment, he reached down and twisted her clit and it sent her over the edge.

When they both had finished, Preston stood back laughing.

"You two," he said, "are trouble."

Colby pulled out of Kalie and stood back, catching his breath.

"When are you going to tell me what happened to you," she said, gazing at him. "Sometimes I think the reason you like to be in control is because somewhere in time, you didn't have any. When are you going to be honest with me? You don't scare me. Nothing you say will frighten me away."

Gasping for breath, he turned and stared at her. "Yes, I never had control when my father beat the shit out of me or my stepfather put his cigarettes out on me. Is that what you want to hear?"

"Release me," she said as she gazed at Preston.

Quickly he undid the ropes so her feet could touch the ground once again. She walked over to Colby and wrapped her arms around him.

"No child should ever have to endure that torture. No one. But what caused you to steal a car and run away?"

Hanging his head, he sighed. When he raised his head, he glanced at Preston and then at Kalie.

"I was eighteen years old. In two weeks, I would graduate from high school and I had every intention of joining the Navy. I liked boats and thought the military would be a great place for me to be able to get an education. A college degree. On this night, my mother was not home, she was working. My stepfather, God knows why she married him, was a drunk."

Preston watched his friend's face as the memory seemed to reach up and grab him. His face contorted. "I had a girlfriend. No, we weren't serious, but we hung out together. I wouldn't let her come over because I'd seen the way he looked at her and it frightened me."

Oh, no…

"But I shouldn't have worried. You see, it was me he wanted to have sex with. He tried to force me. He held me down on the bed until I reached for a bottle and slammed it against his head. We fought, and he kept saying over and over 'That's right boy, fight me. Make it better for me.' I could feel his dick pressing into me and I felt just gross. Disgusted. Sick. I grabbed the lamp and I smashed it against his head. It was enough to daze him and I pushed him off me. But then he came after me and I ran out the door."

Colby put his head in his hands. "I didn't know what to do so I ran. He jumped in the car and came after me. He was going to run me over. Finally, I went into an ally and I jumped into a car and I hot-wired it and took off."

He sighed. "You'd think I would get away from him, but no. It was the chief of police's personal vehicle. He crashed into it and when he did, the police surrounded the car. No one wanted to hear my side. I got three years while he walked the streets of New Orleans a free man."

Shaking his head, he sighed. "My mother came to the jail and told me I was disgusting for accusing her husband of trying to molest me. After the sentencing, I never heard from my mother again."

Turning to Kalie, he gazed at her. "So, yes, I don't deserve a woman like you. It's why I keep trying to push you away. It's why I need control because I have never had much control of my life. So you need to stay away from me. I'm bad news."

Kalie pulled him deeper into her arms. She held him tight.

"Colby, no. You were eighteen years old. You've never had a chance at a good life. But you have one now and nothing you can tell me will send me running. Deep inside, I know you're a good man. I see it every day in the way you treat me and others. I'm not walking away."

Preston walked over and they pulled Colby into a hug. "We'll always be here for you, Colby. Always."

This afternoon something had shifted between them and Preston wasn't certain what. It wasn't Colby's story. Yes, that had been heart wrenching, but there was a difference in Kalie.

The woman oozed with confidence and he saw in her eyes a certainty he'd not seen there before.

CHAPTER 14

"It's been a hell of a day and I'm hot," Kalie said. "I'm going in the air-conditioned house, take a bath, and then I'll be waiting for you. It's time that both of you took me at the same time."

Mouth gaping, Colby watched her pick up her clothes and then scramble down the ladder.

She was the one pushing that they both take her and she wanted it tonight. He feared this meant she was leaving soon. The deal was done, and she would be returning to New York.

Damn, double damn. And this was after he'd told her things that he'd never mentioned to anyone. After he went to prison, he gave up and locked that night away.

With a sigh, he watched her go into the house.

"Let's grab a shower and then go on over," Preston said.

Colby glanced around at the hay they had left to move.

His heart wasn't in it tonight. Glancing at his watch, he realized it was only four o'clock. It was early.

"Maybe we should offer to take her out to dinner," Preston said. "Maybe then she would tell us what happened at the lawyer's."

Colby sighed. "All right. But first I want a shower. I'm hot and sweaty and I want tonight to be perfect."

Why he had such a bad feeling, he didn't know, but he feared she would soon be going back to the Big Apple, never to return to Blessing. And that made his chest ache.

It wasn't what he wanted at all.

Thirty minutes later, he walked into the house. Preston was still getting dressed. Kalie was nowhere in sight. It was then that he saw the paperwork lying on the table alongside her purse.

Unable to resist, he opened the folder. The amount Jim White was willing to pay for this place was staggering. He'd never seen that much money.

"Son of a bitch," he said as he flipped through the pages of the contract. And then his heart stopped when he saw Jim's signature.

She'd sold him the place. It was a done deal. That jerk had offered her enough money that she couldn't refuse him.

And could he really blame her? She'd be set for life.

Just then Preston walked through the door. "Where's Kalie?"

"I don't know," he said, his emotions gripping him. "She sold the ranch."

Preston glanced at the contract.

"I really hoped she would see through Jim White, but he offered her three million fucking dollars."

Rage filled him and he closed his eyes. "I can't do this. I can't fuck her when I know she didn't give a rat's ass about us."

After everything, she had sold them upriver. He didn't even know if they were going to be getting the bonuses that Lillian promised them. Once again, he'd started to care about someone and they had screwed him over.

Preston sighed and shook his head.

"I was praying that she would stay," he said.

Just then Kalie walked down the stairs, wearing the sexiest negligee he'd ever seen, but he didn't care.

"What are you doing?" she asked when she saw them rifling through the contract.

"You bitch, you sold us out," Colby said.

"What? No," she said her face confused.

"It's right here in this contract. Jim White is getting the Sweet B Ranch. He's going to make it into a subdivision with ranchettes. He's the biggest jerk in town and you sold Will and Lillian's ranch to him."

Her face started to turn red.

"It's my decision," she said. "I inherited this ranch."

"Yes, it's your decision," Preston said. "We were just hoping for a better outcome."

"At least we hoped you would sell it to someone who loved the place and would care for it as much as your grandparents did," Colby said as he paced the floor. "I knew better than to get involved with you. You're nothing like Lillian. You're just a snooty bitch from New York City who had no idea the value of the property she'd inherited. Why is it the lucky ones get an inheritance?"

She hurried down the stairs and she stomped toward Colby. "Look here. I'm not a snooty bitch, and I didn't know my grandparents because my father was a jerk to Lillian and Will. And it's my inheritance. I'll do what the hell I want with it."

Preston sighed and walked over to Kalie. "We were hoping you would want to stay and be with us. We're disappointed. I wish you would have told us when you first got home."

A snarl came from Kalie. "Get out. And don't come back. We're done," she said.

"Good," Colby said. "We'll pack our bags and be long gone before that asshole comes to take possession of the ranch. Right now, your grandmother and grandfather are probably rolling over in their graves. Of all people to sell their land to."

Tears welled in Kalie's eyes and she clenched her fists.

"Leave now," she screamed.

He'd never seen her so angry.

Picking up the folder, he tossed it to her. "Enjoy your millions."

Then he turned and stomped out the door, his pulse pounding, rage filling him. He knew better than to get on his motorcycle at this moment because he would take way too many chances.

Somewhere on the road, he would be splattered.

He hurried into the bunkhouse and began to pack his bags. He had to get out of here tonight.

Preston walked in. "I kept hoping she wouldn't sell."

"Well, you were wrong. Jim White will be our new boss."

"Oh hell no," Preston said. "I'm not working for that asshole."

"Me either. In fact, I want to leave tonight. Will you take me into town before the bank closes and let me pull out all my cash? I'm not staying here."

Preston sighed. "Let's go. The bank closes within an hour."

CHAPTER 15

*A*s soon as they walked out the door, Kalie collapsed onto the couch, tears rolling down her cheeks. Didn't they see that she had not signed the contract? Didn't Colby realize that she didn't want to leave?

These were her men. She wanted to remain here with them, but they had believed the worst about her. Maybe she should have pointed out that she hadn't signed the contract, but they had been so mean.

They believed the worst about her and that hurt more than anything.

Well, she wasn't going anywhere and now she was even questioning that decision. She had hoped by staying here that they would eventually commit themselves to one another. But how could she do that if they didn't trust her?

Picking up her cell phone, she started to call them but then put her phone down. She thought about calling

Nathan and decided no. Just no. She wasn't going to make a decision when she was so distraught.

After listening to Colby's story, she'd realized that she loved these men. In the two weeks since she'd been here, she'd fallen in love with them and her heart belonged to them. No one else, and she didn't want to return to New York.

This was where she belonged. But now the question quickly became did they belong here with her?

Sighing, she dialed her friend's number, tears still trickling down her face.

"Stacy," she said when she answered.

"What's wrong? Are you all right? Do I need to call the police?"

"No," she said sobbing. "I don't know what to do."

For the next ten minutes, her friend listened to her. When Kalie told her how Colby had reacted to the contract, she growled into the phone.

"Does the man not know that a contract is not good until both parties have signed? Good grief, this is basic law."

But Colby had never been exposed to contracts, she realized. No, she wasn't making an excuse for him, but Preston should have seen there was only one signature on that contract and it wasn't hers.

"Stacy, what am I going to do? I love them. I thought I had found two men I wanted to spend the rest of my life with, and now I'm wondering if I made the right decision."

Sitting on the couch, she gazed about the house.

"Take a deep breath. There has been enough emotional reaction for one evening. You said they were leaving."

"Yes," she said. "I heard Preston's truck leave about thirty minutes ago."

There was silence for a few minutes on the phone. "They're gone for good?"

"Let me check," Kalie said.

She was still in her sexy negligee, but she walked outside and went to the bunkhouse. Colby's motorcycle was still parked under the awning. When she went inside, she saw that they both had pulled out their suitcases and were filling them.

"They're gone, but their suitcases are still here," she said. "Dear God, I hope they're not going to Jim White's residence. Colby will kill him."

As angry as she was that they had not listened to her, she didn't want Colby hurting someone and going back to prison. The man didn't deserve that.

"Let me call you right back. I'm going to call my attorney," she said.

Dialing his personal cell number, she was thankful Nathan picked up right away. "Have you changed your mind?"

Not at all.

"No, but Colby saw the contract and is under the false belief that I am selling the ranch. He and Preston left furious at me. I'm worried for Jim White's sake. I don't want them to hurt him."

Nathan sighed. "Sometimes Preston and Colby can be

damn stubborn. Let me see if I can reach Preston on the phone and find out where they're at."

"Thank you, Nathan," she said. "But don't tell them I'm staying."

He chuckled. "Why do I get the feeling that two men are going to be getting hell tonight for not believing in you."

"You got it," she said. "They assumed and we all know what that means."

Laughter came over the phone. "Kalie, you're going to fit in very well here. I'm glad you made the decision to stay."

"Thank you," she said. "Now go find my men and tell them to get their asses back to the ranch."

She disconnected the line and then called Stacy back.

"He's going to try to find them," she said. "Why are men so damn stubborn?"

Stacy laughed. "I wish I knew."

There was silence for a moment. "I'm happy for you, but I'm so disappointed that you're not coming back to New York."

"I'll miss you, but, Stacy, this is where I belong. I've learned so much about my family."

Kalie returned to the big house and sank down on the couch. She glanced around the room and knew this was home. Yes, she would make some changes, but here was where she wanted to be.

"Your life is going to be so different," Stacy said.

"Yes," she replied. "If I lose my job, my grandmother left me about a hundred thousand dollars plus the ranch. I'm hoping with the cattle and horses, I'll make enough to survive. If not, I could be in trouble."

"Are you in love with Colby and Preston?"

"Yes," Kalie answered, a tear trickling down her face. "That's why them not believing in me hurts so much. All they had to do was ask me, but instead they accused me of selling to Jim White who is the biggest dirtbag in Texas. And then they quit. They quit the ranch and me. How can I get over this?"

There was silence. "Maybe you have to give them the benefit of the doubt. After all, they have been afraid that they were going to lose their jobs. Believe me, when employees know the place is closing, it can get ugly. I've seen it."

Stacy was an employment director at a large manufacturing plant. She'd been laid off at least twice when plants closed.

"But...I love them and I hoped they were falling in love with me as well," she said, realizing how much their defection hurt.

"Maybe they were and that's why they reacted the way they did. Love is not easy, especially when you're afraid."

Kalie thought about her comments. She had planned on a great evening and now it was ruined.

"Stacy, I want you to come visit me," she said. "After I get the house fixed up and all, come out to Texas and stay with me."

The woman laughed. "What are you going to do with your stuff here?"

She sighed. "I don't know yet. I've got some time to make decisions. Right now, I just have to get over feeling like I lost the best thing I've ever had."

"Are you going to be all right?"

"Yes," she said. "No matter what happens with Preston and Colby, I'm staying here."

"Don't welcome them back with open arms," she said laughing. "Make them work for it whenever they return."

There was no problem with that. Kalie was still so mad, she couldn't see straight. And yet, she wanted her men. They were the reason she was staying. That, and the ranch.

"Call me tomorrow and let me know how things are," Stacy said.

"I will. For now, I think I'm going to go to the bedroom and just wait to see what happens."

CHAPTER 16

"*I* was falling in love with her," Preston said as he drove down the highway away from the ranch.

"I've never been in love, but damn, my heart hurts," Colby said. "You had been talking about marriage and I was beginning to think it might be possible. And then this. I'm never marrying."

Unfortunately, it was going to take a long time for Preston to get over Kalie. The memory of her being tied up, hanging in the barn overcame him, and damn, he wanted her. He wanted her to spend every day of her life at his side.

As they pulled into town, Preston glanced over at Colby. The man's jaw was locked tightly and he could see he was just itching for a fight.

"Don't leave tonight," he told him. "Wait and go in the morning."

"I'm not staying at the ranch," he said. "I can't take a chance on seeing her again and thinking how she sold us out. It wouldn't be pretty."

With a sigh, Preston understood. "Let's sleep at my parents' home. They have the room and we can stay out in the barn and get drunk."

"No, I want to put some road between me and Blessing," he said. "I've had it so good here that it's just killing me to know she let Jim White, that asshole, have the ranch we love."

It was killing Preston as well. The look on her face had been furious that she caught them gazing at the contract. She thought they were going to fuck her tonight and then she would tell them that she'd sold the property and was leaving town.

Well, to hell with that. That's not how it was going to work.

He pulled up in front of the bank and they both got out. With the mood that Colby was in, Preston couldn't let him be by himself. The man was itching for a fight and he was afraid he would start one deliberately just to let go of some of his frustration.

They walked inside the Blessing National Bank and were standing in line when the very person that Preston didn't want to see walked into the bank.

Colby hadn't seen him yet and fear spread through Preston.

There was no way they could avoid the man.

With a sigh, he said, "Don't look now, but Jim White just walked in the door."

Colby whipped around and watched as the man went into an office and laughed and talked to the man behind the desk.

"That son of bitch, I'm going to kill him," he said beneath his breath.

"No, no, you're not," Preston said. "He won, we lost, and we have to accept that."

"No, we don't," Colby said as he walked toward the man.

"Colby, stop," Preston said, running after him.

Hell, why was this happening? Of all the people to come into the bank, why did it have to be Jim?

Colby walked into the office, grabbed Jim by the shirt, and spun him around.

"You son of a bitch," he said. "Why are you so damn lucky? She could have sold it to anyone else but you."

Jim's eyes widened and he raised his hands to protect himself from the punch that Colby was about to unleash on him.

"What are you talking about?"

"The Sweet B Ranch. Why Kalie sold it to you, I don't know. You don't deserve it," he said and his arm was back and ready to hit him.

Just then Nathan came running in and grabbed Colby's elbow. "Stop."

"She didn't sell it to me," Jim said. "I offered her a very

sweet deal and she refused. Why? Did she sell it to someone else?"

Confused, Preston stared at Jim. The man appeared to be telling the truth.

"But I saw the signed contract," Colby said.

"I signed it, but she refused," Jim said.

Whirling around to Nathan, they both stared at him and he smiled.

"Did you ask her if she sold the ranch?" Nathan said. "Or did you see the contract and assume that she sold it to Jim."

Like a ton of bricks, it hit Preston. "Oh hell. We assumed, and she was so mad, a nest of hornets would have run from her."

"Gentlemen, it's not my place to tell you anything. I would suggest you talk to Kalie. Ask her questions. See what she has to say."

Jim became indignant. "She didn't sell the ranch to me. I'm out and the only other contract was Zachary McCoy and I don't think she sold to him either."

Shit! Shit! Shit! What had they done?

"Kalie was afraid something like this would happen. If you want to salvage your relationship and keep your jobs, I suggest you get back to the Sweet B and try to talk her off the ledge. She's pretty upset," Nathan said.

How could they have been so stupid? Because they'd been worried she was going to leave. They had assumed the worst about her.

"You might want to ask her what Granny Jones told her today."

Colby glanced at Preston and they both ran out of the bank manager's office.

"Why does it feel like I really screwed this up," he said.

"I thought you said there were signatures on the contract," Preston asked as they hurried out of the bank and climbed into the truck.

"There was," Colby said. "But I don't remember seeing her signature. Only Jim's before I became enraged."

Preston backed the truck out of the bank parking lot and hurried down the street. He pulled into the grocery store.

"What are you doing? We should get home," Colby said.

He glanced at the man he considered his brother. "After this kind of fight, you don't go home empty-handed. We're getting flowers and a bottle of champagne."

Colby nodded. "Let's take home some takeout."

"Go order steak at the restaurant," Preston said. "Once I get flowers and champagne, I'll pick you up."

Colby turned as he was walking down the street. "What about jewelry?"

"Not tonight, but soon," Preston said. Tonight was all about making up for the stupid mistake they'd made.

Why he hadn't checked the contract, he didn't know, but he wouldn't make that mistake again. Not if he wanted to make her his wife. And he did. The sooner, the better. If she wasn't going back to New York, then he had every intention of marrying Kalie.

Tonight might not be the time to ask her, but soon.

CHAPTER 17

*K*alie had cried herself to sleep. At the sound of someone coming into the house, she woke. She'd changed from her sexy nighty to a long T-shirt and panties. No sense in being in sexy clothes when you weren't in the mood.

Listening, she wondered who had entered her home. Grabbing her phone, she was prepared to call the police.

Then she heard their voices. Only problem was she was still so mad at them, she didn't want to speak to them. She wasn't going down to meet them. Screw 'em.

Just then the door to her bedroom burst open and the two men walked in. Colby carried flowers, which didn't fit his personality at all and Preston held a champagne bottle.

"We're idiots," Colby said. "I'm sorry. I didn't let you speak and I didn't listen to you. All I could think was that you had sold everything and we no longer would be here at the ranch. I let my emotions take over and I was wrong. I'm sorry."

Shocked, she stared at him. The man had never apologized and she was stunned to hear him admit he was wrong.

Preston moved in front of her. "Colby is right. We're idiots. All I saw was that Jim White had signed that contract and I was in a haze of anger. I never looked to see if you had signed it. I love you, Kalie. All I could think was that you were leaving us. And I didn't want you to go. To hell with the ranch. You were the one I didn't want to leave."

Her heart clenched.

"I love you too," Colby said. "And that's damn hard for me to admit. I'm scared to death."

She crossed her arms over her chest. "How did you find out that I didn't sell?"

Colby placed the flowers in her arms and then Preston proceeded to tell her what happened at the bank.

Warmth filled her heart, and she knew that no matter what, she would forgive these two men. She loved them with all her heart, and yes, they had behaved like idiots, but they were her idiots.

Colby stepped behind her and Preston was in front. They wrapped her in their arms.

"Do you forgive us?" Colby asked. "It was my fault. The thought of you leaving got to me. Especially after I'd told you the reason I went to prison. I'd been so vulnerable and I thought you were going to desert us."

She leaned back against him and let her fingers trail down his face. "Colby, I love you. Yes, I forgive you. Both of you."

With a sigh, they pulled her in close between them.

"Preston, I was so disappointed in both of you for not realizing that I hadn't signed the contract. After I spoke to Granny Jones, I made the decision that the Sweet B Ranch was staying in the family. My plan was to tell you both tonight and then make love to you. But I can't do it alone. I'm going to need your help."

Preston pressed into her front. "Darling, I'm not going anywhere. I'm yours."

Colby pressed into her back. "Same here. I'm yours."

"I love you both and I couldn't leave you or the ranch," she said.

"How can we make it up to you? We brought flowers and champagne and even steak," Colby said.

"You can love me. That is what you can do to make it up to me. I need to feel your heart beating against mine. I need to know this is probably the first of many fights we'll experience during our life, but that you'll always be here for me."

Colby reached down and lifted her off the floor and carried her to the bed. "Tonight, we're going to show you just how much you mean to us. We're going to show you how much we love you."

"Tonight is all about you," Preston said.

A smile crossed her face and she slowly peeled the T-shirt down her shoulders and slipped her arms through.

Who needed a sexy negligee when she just wanted her men?

"Oh, darling," Colby said.

She bent over. Slowly she spread her butt cheeks and revealed that she had put the last butt plug in to prepare herself in case they came back.

"Damn," Preston said. "She's wearing our butt plug. Tonight is the night."

A little scurry of uneasiness rippled through her.

"It's time to claim her between us," Colby said. "Make certain she knows she's ours and only ours. That we'll always be here for her."

Oh, she knew that with all her heart.

The men gazed at her like they wanted to eat her alive. And she wanted them. God, how she wanted them.

"There is one little thing we need to discuss," Colby said. "I promised you a spanking tonight and I'm still going to give you one."

"I'd be disappointed if you didn't," she said, rising onto her knees and getting into position.

Colby smiled at her. "All right."

"I'm nervous about tonight, but I want to experience you at the same time. Both of you belong to me. Just like I belong to you. No one else."

"No New York boys are going to come searching for you?" Preston asked.

She laughed. "No."

"Darling, we're going to make tonight good for you," Preston promised.

Now they could finally claim her at the same time and she couldn't wait. She could feel the plug stretching and filling her.

Just the feel of it had her breathing heavier as she gazed at her men, wishing they would touch her. Wanting their hands on her body.

"Over my knee, Kalie," Colby said. "I promise to make you feel good."

Kalie lay across Colby's lap.

"I'm going to take you to the edge, but don't you dare come," Colby said as he raised his hand and connected his palm with her rounded cheeks.

Smack!

Preston gripped her breasts in his hands, massaging and twisting her nipples. Explosions of desire came from so many places on her body that she moaned.

"Colby," she cried out, her hands searching for something to grip onto.

Smack, he paddled her again and again in rapid succession.

Another moan escaped.

To change the rhythm, he spanked her first quickly and then slowly and methodically, taking care to make certain her entire ass went from white to a blushing pink.

Preston stood to the side and stroked his long, hard cock. Rubbing the bead of come that spilled from the end, Kalie watched mesmerized.

Then Preston slapped her pussy and fire went straight from between her legs all the way into her center.

"Preston," she gasped.

"That's the kind of spanking I like to give. One that makes you moan. Up on your knees, darling. I'm going to fuck you like you've never been fucked before."

She tilted her dark curls in one direction. "Yes, I want you so badly."

Preston slapped her pussy again, his fingers lingering on her clit, the heat filling her. Oh, how she wanted them both fucking her at the same time.

Each man was unique. Their penises were different and yet she knew each man just from their smell, their touch, and the way they aroused her. They were her men and she wanted no one else.

Preston was more emotional and caring, and she loved to be held in his arms. Colby was a little rougher, but he scorched her with desire and had her wanting him so badly. He liked to spank her and she liked it too.

"Tonight, we're going to claim you together. I'll take your pussy and Colby, your ass," Preston said.

The anticipation of both of them claiming her left her center melting with heat.

Colby swatted her ass, vibrating ripples up the plug sending tingles through her body. She gasped and turned her gaze to him.

He leaned down and kissed her on the ass, running his tongue along the seam of her cheeks. "You're ours. Do you understand?"

"Yes," she whispered. "Make me yours. Take me together."

This was what she needed, what she wanted – her two men to show her they cared. That tonight had been just a big mix-up that had brought out feelings they were all experiencing. Feelings filled with anxiety but left her hungry for her men.

Colby slid his fingers over her folds before he plunged them inside her. When he pulled them out, she could see the wetness. "She's dripping."

"Please let me come," she gasped.

"Not yet, darling, not yet," Preston said.

Sliding beneath her, Preston scooted over until she lay on top of him, his cock nestled between her legs.

"Do you still want to come?"

A smile spread across her face. "Yes. I need both of you."

"We can't wait to fuck you together," Colby said.

Her ass was warm and tingly, but beneath the pain was pleasure that rode her hard. Lying on the bed, she was anxious, and her body ached for her men to fill her. Never in a million years had she dreamed that pleasure could come from pain, and she liked that her men took charge of her and were rough and domineering.

Just the way she liked it. Exactly what she'd been searching for in New York and never found. Colby and Preston liked to show her they were in charge, but she knew all it would take was for her to spread her legs and they would be there.

Never had she dreamed two men could satisfy her in ways she never imagined. All those years of searching and she'd found exactly what she needed right here in Blessing.

Colby rubbed lube over his long hard cock.

Preston's fingers tweaked her nipples, his piercing sapphire eyes gazed into hers. "Are you ready?"

"Yes," she whispered.

"Ride me," Preston demanded.

Gladly, she raised herself until her hands rested on his chest. Leaning on him, she realized the strength of Preston. All man. Powerful and seductive. Her man.

The bed shifted and Colby climbed behind her. His tongue caressed her buttocks as she hovered over Preston's dick, teasing him by scraping along the bulbous head.

Licking his way down, Colby flicked her clit before he sucked it into his mouth. A groan escaped her and she pushed back, needing more of his tongue, but he pushed her toward Preston's cock.

"When I bury my cock deep inside you, I want your pussy to grip me hard. Try to keep me from moving," Preston whispered. "I'm going to fill you completely."

Just the words made her want to slide his cock deep inside her.

She moved above Preston and then slid down over his hard cock, piercing her eager, wet pussy. At the feel of him, she leaned back as she went lower and lower until she hit his pelvis.

"Preston," she groaned. "You're so deep."

The feel of his long, hard cock snug in her pussy was almost enough to send her over the edge. The plug in her ass was tight against him.

Was this how it would feel when they were both inside her?

All the pleasure from before returned like a stampede battering her with greedy lust. She gasped. Filled with cock and the plug, she was so full, so tight, and yet she wanted more.

She wanted Colby.

Glancing back at him, she gasped, "Where are you?"

He slapped her on the ass. "I'm coming."

She slid up and down on Preston's rigid member, rubbing her clit, needing to ride the pleasure building inside her.

Colby's hand caressed her buttocks, his hand rubbing her ass, pressing her toward Preston.

Preston gripped her face, his mouth descended onto her lips and his tongue exploded into her mouth as his lips demanded that she surrender. A moan escaped her as their tongues tangled, and still, she wanted more.

She needed both of her men. Inside her now.

Colby teased her with the butt plug, pulling and shoving, stretching her that last little bit. Though it felt unnatural at first, now she couldn't wait to experience his meaty cock inside her ass. With both of them inside her at the same time, she would be so full and stretched.

And she would truly belong to them both.

A shallow breath escaped her as he pulled the plug from her ass with one hand while the other one fondled her clit. When the plug came free, she felt opened wide, empty, and bereft.

"Colby, please fuck me."

Leaning over, she felt the flared head of Colby's hard cock press against her trained ass. Slick and hot, the pressure of his invasion grew. Slowly he pushed his rock-hard cock into her. Gasping out loud, her muscles quivered with submission as he filled her, stretching her.

"Aargh," she cried.

"Relax, honey. Let me in," Colby told her.

She took a deep breath and slowly released it, willing her body to stretch and accommodate Colby's cock.

He was big and she had to breathe through her nose and remind herself to relax to accommodate him in her ass. She'd never felt anything so tense, so exhilarating, and so passionate.

With both of them in her body, she felt like there was no room. And yet, her body surrendered, the tight ring of muscle giving way as his cock slid deep inside her. When he was completely in, he paused letting her adjust to the feel of him.

Leaning forward, he whispered against her ear. "Now you're ours. We're claiming you as one."

Both of her men were now inside her body, and she was completely filled.

"Squeeze me, Kalie," Colby gasped.

When she clenched her muscles, she felt as if she were attacking and holding both men hostage. And yet, she'd never felt more passion or more love between them.

Taking a breath, she moaned as Preston moved in

farther, then retreated, the feel of him hard and thick and so wonderful.

A hot rush of desire raced through her as she accepted him into her body, loving the feel of both men. Pinned between them, she whimpered at how they controlled her completely. They began to move, and she gasped, crying out at the rush of feelings.

First, Preston, then Colby, each pushing her closer and closer to the edge as they retreated and filled her over and over. Between them, they maneuvered her body, bringing them all to the brink of pleasure.

Preston pounded into her with Colby retreating. Between these two men was where she belonged. Here was her life. She needed the two of them to fuck her. To claim her. To make her theirs.

They were her men, her lovers. And she couldn't live without them.

"Please, can I come?" she cried, knowing she couldn't hold out much longer.

"Come all over my cock," Preston gasped.

"Milk my cock. Take it deep and squeeze it," Colby cried.

With a bright burst of light, a scream tore through her throat as she squeezed and held her men, working the seed from their bodies. They were hers and she was theirs.

Pleasure filled her and their hot come coated her insides. First, Preston, and then Colby, as they held her between them, their cocks buried deep inside her.

No barriers remained between them. They had marked

her, made her theirs. And joy filled her at the thought of their life together.

This was the life that her grandmother had lived, and now she hoped that soon, they would ask her to marry them, and they would live the same type of life. Nothing would please her more.

Breathing heavily, they reluctantly pulled free from her. Slowly, they returned to normal, but she knew nothing would ever be the same. Her life with her men was not perfect, they would argue again, but it was close to being the life she'd dreamed of for years.

"I love both of you," she whispered as she lay between them. "You've shown me a new way of life that I didn't know existed. You've made me so very happy."

Preston reached out and stroked her hair. "Kalie, until I realized we might lose you, I didn't know how much I loved you. You make us very happy."

Colby held her tightly. "Yes, we love you. I don't know how to have a good relationship. You're going to have to help me create the life I want. The life I'm certain I can have with you."

She raised her head and gazed at them. "You've made my life complete. Now, did someone say there was steak downstairs? I'm starving. Let's go eat."

Rising from the bed, Colby popped her on the ass. "We've turned a bad day into a glorious one. Thank you."

CHAPTER 18

*S*tacy stared at her friend. She'd never seen her happier. The lucky bitch had just married her men and she understood why Kalie was happy. The ranch was wonderful. Her husbands were so damn handsome, it was unbelievable.

It had taken her a while, but now Kalie had everything she'd ever wanted except for a family, and from the way they acted like rabbits, that should be happening soon.

A man walked up beside her.

"Ma'am, I need you to come with me," he said.

Turning she gazed at him, her brows raising. "Whatever for?"

"You're under arrest," he said.

She started laughing. "Did Kalie put you up to this?"

"No, ma'am," he said. "I work with the Texas Rangers and I've been watching you undercover."

"Well, good for you," she said laughing. "I haven't done

anything wrong. I'm not going with you. Besides, this is my friend's wedding. I'm waiting to catch the bouquet and then I'll be getting into my rental car and going back to San Antonio for the night. Tomorrow I fly back to New York."

The man sighed. "Are you coming with me or not?"

"No," she said.

The man had on a suit coat and a dark hat, and his emerald eyes were dusky.

Just then a second man walked up. "Is she the one?"

"She's our perp," the man said.

"Are you guys serious?" she said.

They surrounded her and then she felt the slip of the handcuffs on her wrist.

"Hey," she said.

"Let's go," the man in the dark hat said.

"I want to see a badge."

Suddenly a man stepped out of the shadows in front of them.

"What are you doing?"

The two men grinned. "Having fun."

"Let her go," he said. She gazed at him, he had the most gorgeous head of hair with streaks of gray in it. His eyes were an intense shade of jade. And from what she could see beneath his suit coat, there were hard rigid muscles.

She felt the handcuffs being released and the two young men grinned.

"We meant no harm, it's just a prank we like to play," they said.

"Get out of here," the man told them.

After they were gone, she glanced at him.

"Sorry about that. They're my younger brothers. They get into mischief."

Stacy gazed at the man. "And who are you?"

"I'm Luis Nash, Preston's older brother," he said. "I just got home from the Navy. I own the Rocking B Ranch."

Just then another man walked up beside him. "Who is this?"

"Stacy Rivera," she said. "I'm Kalie's friend."

"Trevor Garcia," the man, said his dark eyes skimming over her, sending a ripple of desire through her.

Those dark brown eyes were filled with sexual heat. A heat she would love to explore.

"You were the maid of honor," Luis said as he moved a little closer.

"Yes," she replied. Glancing at the two of them, her heart beat a little faster. There was something so damn attractive about these two handsome cowboys.

She'd been here a week and during that time, she'd learned so much about this little community. And she was curious about what happened between a woman and two men.

"I guess our little town is quite shocking to a woman from New York City," Luis said.

Shaking her head, she sighed. "No, it's made me curious. I want to learn more about this life. I'd like to experience two men at once. I'd like to learn more about living this way."

Why was she telling them this? She couldn't believe those words had just come from between her lips.

The two men glanced at each other.

"Where are you spending the night?" Luis asked.

"At a hotel in San Antonio," she replied thinking of the two-hour drive ahead of her.

"Do you really want to experience two men at the same time?" Trevor asked.

"Yes," she said, knowing this was her opportunity to experience what she'd only imagined. "I'd like to spend a week being shown what this life is like. For someone to teach me the ropes."

The two men surrounded her.

"We'd like to show you," Trevor said.

"Can you stay another week?" Luis asked.

Her heart leaped into her throat. The smell of each man drifted to her nose and she closed her eyes, inhaling their scents. She might be fired from her job, but she didn't care.

"Yes," she gasped.

"And you want to learn," Luis said. "Because once you come home with us, you're ours for the week. You do understand what you're getting into?"

Her heart thudded in her chest. Was she really going to do this?

"Yes," she gasped. "Yes, Kalie told me."

"Take your panties off," Trevor said.

"Right here? Now?"

"Yes, now," Luis demanded.

Swallowing, she wondered what she'd just agreed to.

"No commitments," she asked, reaching up under her skirt and pulling her underwear down.

"None," they both replied.

"Will you both be sleeping with me?"

"Yes," they both answered.

"Time to leave," Luis said, taking her by the arm. "Time to take you home and fuck you."

Oh, dear, there would be no preliminaries. No warm-up or let's get to know each other.

"Let me tell Kalie good-bye and then I'll follow you to your ranch," she said.

"I'll drive your car," Trevor said. "You ride with Luis."

What the hell was she doing? She'd never been so bold, but then again, maybe this was what she'd been waiting for.

Kalie had found her happily ever after here in Blessing. Maybe she would too.

Come Home to the Ranch Available At All Retailers

OUR FUGITIVE BRIDE

*I*da Newton, matchmaker extraordinaire, stared at the letter in her hand. Winter was ending and it was always a struggle to keep her business going during this slow time. Years ago, after her husband died, she'd become a mail-order bride matchmaker.

And she loved her job, except when the cash grew low. This year, she was barely surviving.

The city of Charleston had slowly recovered from the war, but in the year of our Lord, 1875, people were still struggling. And men from the west were still looking for brides to keep them warm at night.

"Sweet pickles and fresh juniper," she exclaimed, staring at the words on the page, unable to believe her good fortune.

"What?" her assistant asked.

"They want me to find eight women to go to Treasure Falls, Montana, as mail-order brides."

A check slipped out of the folded letter and she gasped. The sum on that piece of paper was almost two years' worth of living expenses.

Sweet hallelujah! Today was her lucky day.

"Oh my," she said, sinking down into a chair. "They're paying me upfront and it's almost double what I would normally receive."

It seemed too good to be true. How had the man heard about her ability to put couples together? Her reputation as a mail-order bride locator was well known in the south, but the west?

Her assistant picked up the check and gasped. "Ida, this is what you are needing. Business has been so slow. This will keep things going. You won't have to sell your house. We can stay in business."

Quickly she scanned the letter and frowned. What woman in her right mind would accept such an offer? What woman on God's green earth would think this was acceptable?

And yet, oh, how she needed this money, but there was no way...

With a sigh, she shook her head. "I can't do it."

"Why not?"

"There are certain conditions."

Suzanne leaned forward. "What conditions? Whatever they are, we will overcome them."

How could she send women out west to be basically a concubine for not one man, but two? She still believed in love and marriage and helping couples find one another, but not two men.

"They share their women. There are two men for every woman."

Her assistant leaned back and howled with laughter. "You're right. No woman would accept such an arrangement."

She glanced down at the letter. "The whole town lives this way. He says there is so much danger that the thought of a woman and his children being left to fend for themselves was too much. The men were afraid they would starve or be forced into other unseemly occupations. Years ago, this mining town made the decision that every woman would marry two men. That they would share her. Then if one man died, she had another man to continue their life together."

Laughter bubbled up from Suzanne. "Maybe it's not as bad as it sounds. If one man was a bad lover, maybe the other one would be a good one. Or you could have two great lovers."

"Suzanne. The very thought of two different men as your husband and lover is…" Ida shook her head. "What decent woman here in town is going to agree to that type of arrangement?"

A sigh escaped from Suzanne. "If I was younger, I might."

Ida shook her head. "No, they will laugh at me. I thought we were going to have a good start to spring. I'll have to send him his check back."

She laid the letter down and Suzanne picked it up.

"Wait a minute. He says that if the women arrive in Treasure Falls and they don't like the area or the people, they will pay for them to return home. It says they will have two weeks to make up their minds and if this town is not for them, they can take the next stage home."

A little flutter of excitement filled Ida's chest. Could she convince women to travel so far west?

Suzanne grinned at her. "It's a long ride home."

"What if I didn't tell them everything and let them decide when they arrive. Let's face it, most of these girls are not coming from ideal situations. They're either alone or helpless or there is some reason they have not found a man here in town."

So many of her young women were running from a bad family life. There were reasons why they had not found a husband. As much as she didn't want to take this man's money, she needed the funds in order to eat.

Her assistant sat back and smiled. "We could be helping them find a good home with not one man, but two to care for them."

Suzanne smiled and gave a little giggle. "Two men. It's hard enough to please one. How do they make love? One at a time or two on one? Oh, I wish I were a fly on a wall. This I would like to see."

"Suzanne," Ida said in a warning tone. "That's...not seemly. We shouldn't think such thoughts."

"Maybe not, but I'm curious about how this would

work. So are we taking on this project or are we going to starve?"

Honestly, she had no choice, but it would be better to let the women decide once they arrived in Montana. Somehow she would just forget to tell them that they would be marrying not one, but two husbands. She hated lying to them, but it was that or find herself out in the street.

Leaning back in her chair, Ida smiled at her assistant. "We've got our work cut out for us. I've got to find eight girls. Load them up on a train to St. Louis and then they will take a boat to Fort Lewis and from there not one, but two stages, will take them to Treasure Falls. A three-month journey from Charleston to Treasure Falls."

For a moment, they each sat in thought.

"It could be a great beginning for these women."

"It could be hell," Ida said. "Oh, goodness, I wish I could tell them what they were getting themselves into, but no one would take the chance. And it's obvious the man has money. They could be living a very rich life."

"This man must be very wealthy for him to request eight women and to pay for their travel and your fee," Suzanne said.

It was true. The amount he was paying her was double what she normally received and he'd sent enough for passage for eight women as well.

But was she being devious not telling these ladies what they were about to get themselves into?

What choice did she have?

This would save her business. It was either that or find another job and the ones available to women were not good.

With a sigh, she grinned at Suzanne, her decision made.

"Where should we start looking?"

"Let's start with some posters on poles spread throughout the city."

Two days later as Ida was hanging up a poster, a beautiful young woman approached her. Her eyes were red rimmed and she looked nervous.

"How can I sign up?"

Ida had her first customer and she gazed at the girl in shock. She was stunning. Her long black hair and emerald eyes that peeked from beneath long dark lashes made even Ida's heart swoon.

How had the men of Charleston missed this woman? Or did she have a secret?

"I'll sign you up."

"When does the journey begin? I have no place to stay and I'm needing to leave right away."

Long ago, Ida had made a decision not to ask too many questions of these girls. There were so many reasons for them becoming a mail-order bride and a lot of them were not good. The less she knew, the better. That way, when their suitors or fathers came looking for them, she could deny any knowledge of why the women chose to leave.

"As soon as I can find eight women. I'm hoping in the next two weeks," she said, thinking that would be nearly impossible, but she would do her best. The longer it took her, the more someone might find out what kind of town Treasure Falls was. "You're welcome to stay at my place until all of you depart."

Years ago, she'd built on several bedrooms for just this type of problem.

"I can't leave now?"

As much as she'd like to say yes, it would be safer for the ladies to be in a group. And the men were expecting all eight at once.

"No, I like my girls all traveling together to protect one another," she said. "Are you interested?"

The woman glanced toward the train station and then back at Ida. "Yes, I would like to become a mail-order bride."

Ida wanted to dance a jig right there in the street but knew that would attract a lot of attention. One down and seven to go and she'd just put up the signs.

She picked up the woman's suitcase and took her by the arm. "What's your name, dear?"

"Mary," she said. "Mary Beattle."

"Well, Mary, I've been doing this a long time and I'm thrilled to help you find a husband. Let's get back to the office and sign the paperwork. You are a virgin, dear?"

"Yes, ma'am," she said.

"Good. From what I've heard about Treasure Falls, Montana, you're going to love it."

Tears appeared in the girl's eyes and Ida wondered about her story.

"I hope so," she said as they walked down the street with Mary looking over her shoulder every few minutes.

With every mail-order bride, she always hoped they found happiness. Even the girls going to Treasure Falls.

Available at All Retailers!

PLEASE LEAVE A REVIEW

Did you enjoy the book? Reviews help authors. I would appreciate you leaving a review at the retailer of your choice.

Follow Lacey Davis on Facebook.

Sign up for my https://laceydavisauthor.com/mailing-list **and receive a free book.**

Also By Lacey Davis

Blessing, Texas Series
Loving My Cowboys
Two Cowboys' Christmas Bride
Two Cowboys One Bride
Two Cowboys Too Perfect
Two Cowboys to Protect Her
Two Cowboys Save Christmas
Box Set 1
Box Set 2

Bridgewater Brides World
Their Perfect Bride
Their Tempting Bride
Their Scandalous Bride
Box Set

RIDE — Rural Intergalactic Defense Enforcement
Before They Came to Earth
Hunter's Heart, Alien's Kiss #1
Hunter's Heart Rebel's Touch #2
Hunter's Heart Alien's Vow #3

The Magic Mirror Series
Cauldron Academy
Enchanted Deadline
Witch's Wrath

Curse of Destiny Falls
Matrimony & Magic
The Matchmaker's Mission
Box Set

Return to Blessing, Texas
Come Home to the Cowboys
Come Home to the Ranch
Come Home to the Lawmen
Come Home to the Country
Come Home to the Doctor's
Come Home to the Bride
Return to Blessing, Texas Books 1-3
Return to Blessing, Texas Books 4-6

Treasure Falls Brides
Our Fugitive Bride
Our Desperate Bride
Our Wild Bride
Our Dangerous Bride
Our Lucky Bride
Our Christmas Bride
Box Set 1
Box Set 2

Want to learn about my new releases before anyone else? Sign up for my New Book Alert and receive a complimentary book. Blindfold Me.

Lacey Davis is the *alter ego* of a USA Today, bestselling author who decided to dive headfirst into the world of sexy romance. Why? Because who doesn't love writing about hunky bad boys and fierce, fabulous women who know how to make them beg for more? With these sizzling stories, I'm here to deliver the kind of romance that will leave you reaching for a fan (or an ice bath—your choice).

If you're into bad boys who like to take charge and strong women who aren't afraid to shake things up, then you've come to the right place. These steamy reads will not only get your pulse racing but also have you cheering for these bold women as they tame their wild men—and leave them wanting more. Ready for a little fun? Come on in, the temperature's *just* right.

www.LaceyDavisAuthor.com
The End